PUFFIN BOOKS

OUR KID

25p

A paper round at last. It's the chance Frank's been looking for, to earn some money and do up the basement as his own private room. No more sharing with 'Slob', his older brother Malcolm. And it might even give his lonely, unemployed father a reason to be proud of him.

But to his surprise, Frank discovers another side of Darnley. In the poshest part of the town he meets the wealthy Manning-Sanders family – Tim, with his fabulous bedroom, and his gorgeous sister Cassie. At next-door's convent he strikes up an unlikely friendship with Sister Maggie, always good for a laugh, but always doing things for down-and-outs like old 'Smelly Eric'.

Then there's the man with the birthmark. Could such a polite and respectable-looking type really be the burglar responsible for the recent spate of break-ins? The mystery deepens as he embarks on his 'research' into back numbers of the local papers for the school's 'Our Town' competition. But in a surprising and moving climax, he gains new insight into the extraordinary things people will do for love.

This marvellously readable and richly plotted novel is everything one expects from this *Guardian* Award-winning novelist.

Ann Pilling was brought up in industrial Lancashire where many of her books are set, but has also lived in Wales, London, Buckinghamshire and on the East and West coasts of the USA. For some years she taught English, but has been writing since 1979. She now lives in Oxford with her family – one husband, two sons, two cats – and enjoys walking, singing, cooking, music and gardening. Whenever possible she retreats to the Yorkshire Dales.

OUR KID

ANN PILLING

PUFFIN BOOKS

PUFFIN BOOKS

Published by the Penguin Group
Penguin Books Ltd, 27 Wrights Lane, London W8 5TZ, England
Viking Penguin, a division of Penguin Books USA Inc.
375 Hudson Street, New York, New York 10014, USA
Penguin Books Australia Ltd, Ringwood, Victoria, Australia
Penguin Books Canada Ltd, 2801 John Street, Markham, Ontario, Canada L3R 1B4
Penguin Books (NZ) Ltd, 182–190 Wairau Road, Auckland 10, New Zealand

Penguin Books Ltd, Registered Offices: Harmondsworth, Middlesex, England

First published by Viking Kestrel 1989
Published in Puffin Books 1991
1 3 5 7 9 10 8 6 4 2

Printed in England by Clays Ltd, St Ives plc
Filmset in Palatino (Linotron 202)

OUR KID

Chapter One

It was seven o'clock, nearly dark outside, and Frank sat by the gas-fire having a quiet read. The house smelt of Friday night, fish and chips and the warm greasy newspaper they'd been wrapped in. It was his favourite smell and Friday his favourite night, Gala Night, when Slob stayed over at Lesley's.

On the table a fat oozy meringue sat in a box. Dad had eaten his already, with his chips. *Yuk.* Frank's was still untouched, smug in its frilly white paper; he liked keeping his treats to the end. They only had meringues on Fridays and then only if Slob was out. He said it was no use moaning on about money if you went round spending it on fancy cakes. It was all right for him, he'd got a good job.

Slob was Frank's nineteen-year-old brother. He never called him Frank, just 'you', or 'our kid'. His own name was Malcolm and that's what you had to call him these days. He wouldn't answer to 'Malc' any more; he was dead touchy. In private, though, Frank had christened him Slob, alias Malc the Mok, just to get his own back.

His head was shaved except for the bit on top and he'd turned that into a bright red crest six inches high, starting low on his forehead and running half-way down his back. He looked as if he'd escaped from the Roman Life section of Darnley Municipal Museum.

Lesley was a mohican as well. Her current hairdo was

yellow spikes with bright purple make-up. Together the pair of them resembled a couple of man-eating insects out of a late-night horror movie. Lesley was fat, with legs like bananas. Malc's girlfriends were always on the large side.

Still, if it wasn't for her, Frank wouldn't have this peace and quiet with Dad. He even had the bed to sleep in tonight. Normally, Malcolm slept in it and Frank had to kip down on the lumpy Put-U-Up with his feet sticking out over the end. Sharing a bedroom with Slob was the thing Frank hated most about his entire life.

'Any joy?' Dad grunted from his seat at the table. They were both reading newspapers but his was the one the chips had come in. The grease marks obviously made it difficult and behind his glasses his little round eyes were all screwed up. Everything about Dad was little; little hands, little feet and a little round head, bald and covered with brown splodges like the top of Horlicks. Frank was tall for his age and he towered over him.

Sometimes he got the urge to polish that little round head with a duster; not tonight though, Dad seemed rather depressed. It was probably because he'd still not heard from the bank.

'Come and talk to us' the TV advert had said. 'No project is too small for our listening ear, we may well be able to provide the loan you need. Make that castle in the air a castle on the ground. Just drop in for a chat with your Friendly Northern Bank manager. We're the little one, so we try harder.'

Dad didn't go in for 'chats', he was too shy. Instead he'd written them a letter explaining his idea and asking them to lend him a few thousand pounds. He wanted to set up his own electrical business at home. Their front room was quite big but jam-packed with the stuff people brought round for repair. On top of that there was the stuff he got himself through the small-ad columns in the local papers.

Since he'd lost his job with Morland's Electrical, the

8

money from those repairs had just about kept them ticking over. It wasn't enough though; he needed a proper workroom at the back and a real shop with a counter and a till. Their front room would be just the place for that.

Frank was all for it. They never used the room anyhow and it'd be great to have real money coming in again after two years scratching and scrimping. But the Friendly Northern Bank hadn't replied yet and Mr Tanner was getting gloomier and gloomier. 'Any joy?' he repeated, folding up his own greasy sheets and staring at Frank's meringue. 'They've made enough fuss about that new paper. Anything worth going for?'

The 'new paper' was called the *Denning Spotlight*. It had only been out two weeks and it was free. There wasn't much news in it, just rows and rows of advertisements. Denning was the poshest part of Darnley where all the big houses were, on the edge of the golf course. Dad was obviously hoping to pick up some high-quality stuff to repair and resell.

Frank looked down a long column headed 'Under £20'. 'Brownie Dress and Hat,' he volunteered. 'Hardly been used. £4 or nearest offer.'

'You what?'

'Wedding Dress, wild silk, size 20. Never been worn.'

'Frank, what are you playing at?' Mr Tanner wasn't in the mood for jokes.

'Sorry, Dad. OK, here we are. Electrical . . . electrical . . . "Hoover Spin-drier, £15, needs slight attention." What about that? "Steam iron, still boxed, unwanted gift, only £8." '

'That sounds more like it. Chuck it over and I'll mark them, then I'll make a few phone calls.'

'Hang on a minute.' Frank was gripped now. The *Spotlight* was bursting with goodies. 'Ladies Romance Novels,' he spelt out, '65 for £10. Will separate.' He went off into a little dream, just thinking about it. Somewhere, in one of those massive houses overlooking the golf course, a fat lady sat abandoned in her wild silk wedding dress, reading romance novels and weeping over her unwanted steam iron. Perhaps that brownie outfit had been hers too, when she was little. There was a whole new world in the pages of the *Denning Spotlight*.

'I'll have that meringue if you can't manage it,' Dad said.

Frank couldn't, his fried cod had been a whopper and he was full up. He gave Dad the *Spotlight* and pushed the cake box across the table.

Dad was always going on diets because he had a sweet tooth and got fat easily. He was so short he was starting to look a bit of a comic, all belly and bum. He'd be as broad as he was tall soon, like the walking sugar lump on that telly advert.

Frank glanced at him, guiltily wolfing the meringue and going down the £20 column with his red biro. The daft thing was that his current bedside reading was a health book from Boots called *Flatten That Stomach!* It prescribed 'graduated and safe exercises for men over 40 who want to regain their youthful vigour and fitness.'

When he'd spotted it he'd wondered if there was a woman around again. Dad got 'ladyfriends' from time to time and he always cheered up then. But Frank hadn't noticed anything happening on that front, and he seemed really fed up tonight. It must be because he'd not heard about his loan from the bank.

'There's a job for you here, son,' he said, ringing something with his red biro. 'It sounds right up your street.'

Frank peered over his shoulder. 'Bright lad wanted for *Spotlight* and other deliveries,' he read. 'Apply Wendy News, 14 South Parade, Denning. Good appearance an advantage.'

His heart did a flip. He'd been trying to get a paper round for ages but someone else always beat him to it. And here one was, for the asking. You were supposed to be thirteen but most paper shops seemed to bend the rules these days. Brian Wilde in their class delivered

10

papers, and so did Amy Chauncey (*paperperson*, she called herself, she was mad on women's rights). Anyhow, neither of them was anything like thirteen. Frank nearly was and he was tall too. That made him look older for a start, and if he combed his hair forwards and borrowed Dad's old glasses, he'd definitely fool them. *A paper round* . . . money in his pocket at last.

Frank needed cash desperately. He only got a bit of weekly pocket money from Dad and sometimes not even that. His father couldn't always spare it and he didn't like asking. If only he had some real money, he could buy things for the front bedroom, make it into a 'den' like they talked about on telly. Getting Slob to move out was the biggest problem. He was always talking about renting his own place but he never actually did anything. Still, if Frank could earn some money it would be a real step on the road to having what he'd always dreamed of, a room of his own. He was *definitely* applying for this paper round.

What would they pay though? Well, South Parade, Denning was quite classy and a classy shop'd probably pay classy rates. 'Wendy News' sounded promising too. In a vision, Wendy came to him, half a head shorter than he was, sweet-smelling and wearing one of those fabulous smocks they sold at Monsoon in King Street. Frank often stopped to look at the bright rugs and wall hangings in their window; he liked beautiful things, and there weren't any in this house.

'But you need to be thirteen, Dad,' he muttered. He felt doubtful, somehow. A posh shop like Wendy's would probably be the sort that stuck to the rules and Dad was always on at him to 'tell the truth at all times'. 'It's the only way, son,' he'd say solemnly, as if telling the truth had made his own life into one big success story. And what was Dad? A lonely, frightened little man whose twin ambitions were to flatten his stomach and start an electrical business in their front room. Frank wanted more than that for his life.

11

'Well, go and see them anyway, you never know. If they're funny about your age there might be something else you can do for them, to earn a bit of spending money.' He seemed rather eager for him to go after this job. Was it because he felt such a flop himself? He'd been so proud when Malcolm had got the job with Qwik-Fit Exhausts. Was he starting to live his life through Frank now?

Oh, Dad. Sometimes he wanted to put his hands round that little bald head and cradle it from all harm.

But he said, 'OK, I will. Mind if I take the paper up with me?'

'Leave page four, I might phone those numbers. You're not going to bed yet, are you?'

'No, I just want to get everything ready. Paper shops open very early. Amy Chauncey starts her round at half past six. I don't want anyone beating me to it. Mind if I have a quick bath?'

'Well, all right, but don't use all the hot water up. Give us a kiss then.'

He bent down and planted one amid the brown Horlicks blodges, then he tucked the *Spotlight* under his arm and went upstairs. Slob said he must be 'queer', kissing his father at his age, but Frank wasn't bothered. He loved Dad and Dad loved him. Slob had Lesley; they'd just got each other.

While the bath was running, he tried to sort the front bedroom out. As he stood in the doorway, looking at all the mess, a wave of complete hopelessness swept over him. Honestly, Slob was worse than a pig in a sty, the way he left his stuff around.

There were dirty clothes all over the floor with books and newspapers dropped on top of them, and tapes and cassette boxes on top of that. In the easy chair some grubby-looking boxer shorts with green handprints on them had obviously got together in the night and bred. A waste-paper basket sat perched precariously on top of a tangled lump of bedding, disgorging its contents over the side and on to the floor: empty cigarette packets and chewed dogends, a squashed McDonald's carton with a solitary chip stuck to the side, all mixed with tomato sauce and little handfuls of Malc's scarlet hair. The sight and smell of the whole thing made Frank's stomach heave.

Once, when he was little, he'd got some chalk and drawn a line down the middle of the carpet. 'You keep to your side and Malc keep to his,' Dad had said timidly. Frank liked things neat and tidy, even then. But Malc had always had moods. 'Tantrums' Dad used to call them, when Malc was Frank's age. Now he just got into filthy tempers.

The chalk line had disappeared years ago, but to Frank it was still there. Wearily he stripped Slob's bed and dumped everything in the dirty linen basket across the landing. Dad went to the launderette on Saturdays and the rule was that you changed your sheets the night before. As he stuffed the last one in, a handful of big black toenails fell out accompanied by a long piece of dried skin. Slob had a delightful habit of picking at his feet before he got into bed, then throwing selected bits at Frank. It was his idea of a joke.

He went back to the bedroom, rammed everything down into the waste-paper bin, then carried it downstairs and out into the yard. If he left it here it'd just sit and stink for another week. Finally he pushed the window up. The smell from outside was foggy Darnley mixed with fish and chips from up the street and diesel fumes from the lorries on Rochdale Road. But it was a whole lot better than Malc's cigarettes; forty a day he got through, half of them in this bedroom.

When Dad whispered 'Cancer' he just laughed. Gran Corcoran smoked a packet a day, and she was pushing seventy-five. That's how thick Slob was, in spite of his good job with Qwik-Fit Exhausts, thinking if it was OK for Gran it was OK for him.

*

13

The bath had started to run cold so Frank did a quick in and out, just long enough to freshen himself up and re-read the Wendy News advert. 'Bright lad wanted' – was he 'bright'? Not particularly, not if it meant schoolwork. He'd be OK, if only the teachers didn't rush him. But it was 'go, go, go' at the Comprehensive, and Frank liked to take his time about things. He was very practical though, good with his hands, and he'd started to help Dad a bit too, wiring plugs and stuff. Brains weren't everything.

He could manage a 'good appearance' anyhow; he'd got clean jeans in his drawer and that sweater Gran had given him for his birthday. He hated the colour, donkey-brown with black jig-jags all over it, but at least it was new and respectable-looking. He'd wear that, and his school lace-ups; they'd give a better impression than his beaten-up sneakers.

When he got out of the bath, he put the *Denning Spotlight* together tidily, glancing at the back page. To celebrate their first month of publication they were running a 'Supermum' competition. Anybody could write in and tell them (in not more than three sentences) why their mum deserved the fifty-pounds prize. 'My mum's the best because she kisses and cuddles me' one kid had written, and there was Mum grinning out at everybody, thirteen-stone plus with her two front teeth missing.

Back in his bedroom Frank cut out the paper-round advert and put it in his anorak pocket ready for tomorrow morning. He didn't much want to look at Supermum competitions. They'd not got a mother.

When he'd told paperperson Amy Chauncey that she'd died when he was born, she had refused to believe him. 'I told my mum,' she said. 'She's a ward sister at Darnley Infirmary and she said people don't die having babies these days.'

'D'you think I'm having you on then?' Inside his trouser pockets Frank had felt his hands bunch together suddenly, into hard fists. It wasn't 'these days' anyhow;

it was thirteen years ago nearly, and it had happened. OK, so he did tell lies now and again, but he wouldn't tell one about this. 'You ask our Malcolm,' he'd told her. 'That's why he hates the sight of me, and why he gets into his rages. If it wasn't for me he'd have a mother like everyone else. You can't blame him, in a way.'

Cleverclogs Amy had gone bright scarlet. 'I'm very sorry, Frank,' she'd stammered. 'I didn't realize . . .'

But somehow he'd been unable to let it go. He wasn't deliberately cruel with people, not like Slob could be, but he just felt like hurting Amy Chauncey. 'That's OK,' he'd said sarcastically. 'You can always come to the cemetery one Sunday, with my dad and me. She's in row ninety-seven, if you get lost.'

Actually, he hardly ever went now, and Slob never did. He'd stopped going for good the day those kids had laughed. Mum's name had been 'Elsie', short for nothing, so the name on the headstone said 'Elsie Tanner'. The kids had pointed and tittered, then run off. It was the same name as that brassy-looking woman who used to be on *Coronation Street*, the one with all the boyfriends.

Malc and Dad had struggled together among the gravestones. 'It's not worth it, son,' Dad had pleaded, trying to stop Malc from pelting after the kids and thumping them. 'Forget it, son, leave them be. Think of your mum, she'd have laughed.' And that had done it. There in the horrible cemetery, with its dog dirt and its litter and its jumble of gloomy memorials, thirteen-year-old Malc had stood and sobbed.

Frank cherished that painful memory. It was the one bit of proof he'd got that his brother was a human being.

Well, he'd not asked to be born and his needs were simple: a clean share of a clean room with nice things in, if he couldn't have one of his own. Slob was never going to get his own flat, and the only unused bit of the house was the cellar. It was certainly private but it was too damp to sleep in. If only the bank would lend Dad money to do it up, as well as giving him the loan for the business.

As he dozed off he dreamed of a basement den all to himself. They could get the old gas-fire down there fixed and it'd be warm then; they could paint the walls white and the woodwork a trendy green or mustard-yellow; they could carpet it, hang pictures up . . . Money was the answer to most things and if he got this paper round it'd be a start. 'Great oaks from little acorns grow' – that was one of Dad's sayings. It was just that his own acorns were a bit slow in coming on.

Frank dropped off to sleep dreaming of Wendy, all willowy and ethnic and smelling of gorgeous soap.

Chapter Two

He had his clean clothes all ready, folded in a neat pile on a chair. The minute his alarm bleeped at half past five, he slid his hand under the pillow and snapped it off. Then he felt round for his clothes, eased the bedroom door open and crept out on to the landing. He got dressed downstairs in front of the gas-fire, then went through to the scullery and let the Flumps in. They thought it was Christmas, the way they came purring and rubbing against his legs. Dad didn't usually feed them till he got up.

It was his father who'd christened them the Flumps, after a telly programme. He liked children's TV. Flump 1 was female and Flump 2 was male. They'd been left on the doorstep of the local chippy one night after closing time – perhaps someone thought a chip shop might take pity on two straggly grey kittens and feed them up with fried cod. But nobody wanted them so Dad brought them home instead. Frank didn't quite know why; it cost money to keep two cats and in a few weeks' time they'd have to have their operations. Slob didn't approve of the Flumps; he said they made the house smell. That was a laugh, coming from him.

Whenever he saw them, he took a sly kick in their direction. But they were quick learners, and at the first whiff of Malc the Mok they always hid under the dresser.

Before setting off Frank arranged cornflakes, teapot,

toast rack and cereal bowls on the table, to make it look homely for Dad when he came down. He left the gas-fire on low too, to keep the room warm. The Flumps immediately curled themselves up into grey fluffy balls in front of it and started to purr like little engines. Cats made a house a home; that's what Dad said anyhow. When he'd got his own room they could curl up on his bed, on a feather duvet. That's what this paper round was all about.

He got his bike out of the shed, swung the back gate open and pedalled off. It wasn't quite six o'clock and he might arrive too early. Still, he could always hang around till they opened. Better than missing the job.

The quickest way over to Denning was across the Larkfield Estate. If he didn't take that route, it'd mean an extra two miles along the dual carriageway that led to the M62. The traffic on that road never stopped, and his father lived in fear and dread of one of them getting squashed on it in some grisly traffic pile-up; Frank had promised never to ride his bike along there. Dad worried all the time about road accidents and he'd sulked for weeks when Slob turned up in his second-hand Renault 4; he'd got it cheap through Qwik-Fit Exhausts, the firm he worked for.

Frank didn't like Larkfield though, it had got a bad name. Not just because Darnley Corporation had put what it called all its 'problem families' into its clapped-out council houses but because, six months ago, there'd been a murder there. An eighty-year-old woman had been found battered to death in her little front garden, all for nine pounds fifty and her pension book. And in spite of the identikit pictures in all the police stations and post offices, the murderer had never been found.

There'd been a horrible photo of the body in the *Darnley Examiner*, and it had given Frank such night-mares that he'd slept with Dad for a bit, in the big double bed.

The road to Denning went straight through the middle,

then climbed up towards the moors that ringed the sooty little town of Darnley-in-Makerfield with all its factories. Anyone with money lived in the leafy suburbs of Denning or Beeswood or Cavendish, and they didn't work in Darnley as a rule, they commuted to Manchester or Leeds.

It was funny that Denning, the poshest suburb of all, sat cheek-by-jowl with this estate. The Denningites wouldn't normally drive home along here though. They'd not want to look at the gardens full of old mattresses, the overflowing dustbins, the four-letter words daubed on every other wall. It was depressing in the early morning sunshine and at night it was a real No Go Area.

Yet Dad could remember when it was all meadows; there'd been a farm on it too, where you could buy milk and eggs. He used to come here with Mum, he said, on summer evenings. Frank looked at the litter, the car tyres in the oily grass, the filth in the gutter, pedalled harder and stared straight ahead, concentrating on the lovely Wendy. No lark could have sung round here for a very long time.

South Parade lay on the other side of Dad's deadly dual carriageway and Frank pushed his bike across, dodging the lorries. The huge road severed Larkfield from Denning as neatly as a surgeon's knife. On one side lay the sprawling estate, on the other Edwardian Denning, huge wedding-cake houses set in vast gardens, broad tree-lined avenues where all was neatness, order, calm. Palace Road, the poshest of the lot, even had a big white gate across it with a notice saying 'No Funerals'. What happened if you died on the wrong side of the gate then, Frank wondered. Did they airlift you to the cemetery? Wendy might know.

When he saw her, though, his heart plummeted, and his mind wandered back to that ad for the size 20 wedding dress. It must be hers; she'd probably got cut-price rates because their shop was doing the *Spotlight*. The bit he could see of her, slumped behind the counter, must weigh thirteen stone at least, and what must her legs weigh, and her bottom? 'Lily Chadwick' it had said over the door and here she was. There was obviously no Wendy any more.

'We're closed,' she brayed, 'can't you read?'

'Yes, I know, only I've come about this,' and he took the *Spotlight* ad from his anorak pocket, unfolded it and laid it on the counter. Then he stepped back, brushed down his jeans, put his feet together neatly and tried to look like a 'bright boy'.

Lily screwed up little pin-ball eyes suspiciously and fingered the scrap of paper, gingerly, as if it was infected. 'Don't know anything about this,' she grumbled, 'where d'you get it from then?'

'The *Spotlight*. It was in yesterday.'

'Huh, well I don't know anything about it. Have to speak to the boss about this.'

She picked up a phone and dialled a number. 'That you, Percy? It's Lil. Listen, I've got a boy here after a paper round. Thought you said we could manage? I – you what? *What*? Yes. No, it's all right, they've arrived. In the back, marking up. So what about this ad then? You what? Oh, all right then. Okey-dokey.'

'Mr Chadwick doesn't come in mornings any more,' she told him, slapping the phone down and lighting a cigarette. 'Dickey heart. He runs the business side though, should've gone into a bank like all these yuppies. He'd have made a small fortune. Good head for figures, my Percy's got. The newspaper deliveries are all on computer now.'

'Er, well is the job still going then?' She didn't seem in the least interested and he was beginning to lose heart. He didn't much want to stand there getting smoke blown over him and listening to the home life of Mr and Mrs Percy Chadwick.

'That depends,' she said, giving him a very hard stare. Frank stared back, he could stare anyone out, it was

20

the thing he was best at, at school. But the minutes ticked. What the stare meant was, How cheaply can we get you for? Possibly, too, How old are you?

'Got any O levels?' she said suddenly.

'Er, not yet.' She must mean GCSEs but he was too young for that.

'Got any EEGs?'

'You mean GCSEs? Well, no, we've not started any of that yet.' EEG? Wasn't that to do with brain scans or something? Didn't they go on about EEGs on those crummy Australian doctor serials Dad watched in the afternoons? *EEG*. Lily Chadwick must be a bit thick. She obviously couldn't run a marshmallow, let alone a paper shop. Come back, Percy, all is forgiven.

'And what's your name then?'

'Frank Tanner.'

'At the Comprehensive, are you?'

'Yes.'

'Like it, do you? Good at your lessons?'

'It's not bad.'

'Hmm . . . well, we've got boys from Bryces' delivering for us. Really smart boys they are, they're in the back marking up.'

Frank had already spotted two of them through a door, pencilling street numbers on piles of newspapers in those flashy black blazers trimmed with red braid. Bryces' was the posh school in Beeswood Park, the school where you had to pay.

Lily was staring at him again through her little piggies, coldly, all set to give him the push; Frank could feel it coming. Then she said suddenly, 'You're not Feargus Tanner's boy are you, out of Bailey Street?'

'Yes, he's my dad. D'you know him then?'

She shrugged, sucked on the drooping fag, and gave a little smile. 'Did do once, me and Perse.'

Well, well, well. Could Lily be one of Dad's old flames? There was an outside chance she might have

21

been pretty once, though it was hard to tell now, under all the layers of flab.

'Tell you what I'll do. I'll have a word with Perse this afternoon and if we *don't* want you we'll ring. On the phone, are you?'

'Yes, Darnley 1198.' It was against Dad's 'rules' to make phone calls; they just had it for 'emergencies'. Dad was nervous in case him or Malc got ill in the middle of the night and they couldn't get a doctor to come. What if one of them fainted in the bathroom and he couldn't open the door? There was no lock on it for that very reason. Only last week Frank had rushed in, desperate for a pee, revealing Malc enthroned on the bog with his jeans round his ankles, reading Judge Dredd. He'd thumped him afterwards, but Dad still wouldn't allow a bolt on the door. Once he'd made up his mind, that was it.

'OK,' and she scribbled the number down. 'If Perse says no, I'll ring.'

'*When*, though?'

'You're keen, aren't you?' The piggies were eyeing him more curiously now, the neatly pressed jeans, the neat hair, the lace-ups placed tidily together, side by side.

'Just want the job, don't I? I need the money,' and a vision of his new room floated before him.

'OK, if I've not rung by ten tonight, it'll mean it's all right. Here, you'd better have a look at this. It's Mr Chadwick's printout for the *Spotlight*. You could have a little ride round, couldn't you, on your way back, then you'll know the route. That's what Bryces' boys always do, when they first start.'

'All right.' Frank took the long roll of computer paper and stared at it nervously. He was rather a slow reader and it was going to take ages to get all these little details into his head. As well as the *Spotlight* some people had weeklies and monthlies, all listed in that funny computer type and a bit faint. Just the sort of thing he'd get

22

all wrong. And the Bryces' brigade, in the back room, were obviously Lily's pride and joy. He had a sinking feeling he'd be compared with them, unfavourably.

'While you're at it you could deliver this for me.' She fished under the counter and produced a dog-eared copy of the current *TV Times*. Cilla Black's cheesy grin stared out at him. 'It's for 105 Palace Road, new customers. It should've gone last week but it got missed. They won't mind, not that sort.'

'OK then.' Frank tucked it under his arm and made for the door, still reading Percy's printout. 103 Palace Road said, 'Manning-Sanders, *Spotlight, Financial Times, Mad, Smash Hits*. 104 said, 'Pearson, *Spotlight, Daily Telegraph*, the *Lady*.' 105 said, 'SLG, *Spotlight, Independent, Radio* and *TV Times*.'

'Not the sort that minded' . . . what could SLG mean? School for Little Girls? Society for Lost Gnomes?

He said, 'What time on Monday, I mean, if you don't phone?'

'Six-thirty, on the dot.'

'Can I mark up as well? I could come earlier?' (They had to pay you extra for that. Paperperson Chauncey had told him.)

'No, Bryces' boys do all the marking up.'

'I see.' One look at her face told him that it was no good asking a second time. Still, it did sound as if his job was more or less in the bag. He'd got Dad to thank for that; she'd definitely changed when she heard he was 'Feargus's boy'.

He climbed back on to his bike feeling quite chirpy, almost a man of the world. *He'd got a paper round at long last*. Perhaps, with his first week's pay, he might buy a big pot-plant to go in the bedroom. It could sit on top of Malc's portable TV.

105 Palace Road had a skip outside and looked a bit sleazy compared with all the other houses. 'SLG' was chalked on the gate-post, crooked. The huge privet

hedge along the front was definitely in need of a good haircut and so were the straggly rose bushes that bordered the weedy gravel drive. The flower beds were full of bottles and empty beer cans and he'd noticed a lot more of them in the bottom of the skip. 105 looked as if it had been a winos' retreat, before the lost gnomes moved in. And that must have been quite recently. There was a 'For Sale' notice dumped under a holly bush.

The front door had a really enormous letter-box, and as he stuffed his *TV Times* through, he peeped into the house. All he could see was a bare, tiled hall with a table to one side of it and an old-fashioned-looking black telephone. The floor and the walls looked very clean and scrubbed. The only other visible object was a row of coat hooks at the far end. He could see seven macs neatly hung up and all were a pale purplish colour. Frank had quite a funny turn when he noticed those. The seven dwarfs were obviously in residence.

Before letting go of the flap, he stuck his ear against the door and had a little listen. Very faint and far away he could hear somebody singing hymn tunes.

Half-way down the path again he collided with an old man; he was a head shorter than Frank and rather ugly. He'd got hard little eyes and a flat nose, with cavernous nostrils always on the twitch. His mouth had a discontented twist to it and the lower lip stuck out so much he could have tripped over it. He was clutching a bottle. 'Anyone in then?' he muttered and a great wash of whisky mixed with onions came out of the enormous mouth.

'Dunno. I didn't see anyone.'

'What you doing here then?'

'I'm the new paper boy.'

'So you've not seen anyone around like?'

'Nope. Someone in there's singing hymns, though, I did hear that.'

'Oh, Gawd. Are they still at it? Never know when to

24

stop, that lot,' and the old man pushed past irritably, taking up a squatting position on the scrubbed front-door step, waving his bottle as if he was waiting for opening time.

103 Palace Road, next door, was an identical wedding-cake house with massive bay windows on each side of the front door, littler bays at all the upper windows and two matching, pointy turret roofs on top, one with a bright green weathercock on it.

Someone obviously cared about this house though. The gravel drive was weedless, the shrubs pruned and the hedge cut close with manic precision. Slowly, trying hard not to crunch on the gravel, he walked up the path.

In front of the drawn curtains the big sash windows shone as the morning sun came up. Only one of them gave him a clue about the inmates. The basement was obviously someone's bedroom with its curtains left pulled back. Below ground level you needn't bother about shutting them. He wouldn't either, when he'd moved into his cellar bedroom.

He wanted to have a dekko into this subterranean room, just to see what they'd done to it. It might give him a few ideas for his own. The house seemed quiet enough, so he squatted down by the front door and stared in.

He could see an empty bed with its jazzy striped duvet thrown back, one of those squishy black armchairs they had in TV plays, and rows and rows of shiny white shelving filled with books and records and tapes. In the middle of the main window hung a huge green fern. It looked great against all the fresh white paint. Frank, thinking of their dark damp cellar under Bailey Street, and the messy room he had to share with Malcolm, felt a sudden stab of envy.

Then he heard water flushing and a boy wandered into the room, pulling his pyjama bottoms up and scratching his head. Frank must have moved his feet slightly because a chip of gravel suddenly pinged against the window and the boy looked up.

They stared at one another. The boy in pyjamas had very tight ginger curls and a pale face sprinkled with tiny freckles. He was quite little, no higher than Frank's shoulder, and Frank should know. It was the new boy in their class and he sat in the next desk.

'What are you doing here?' The window had been pushed up and the fern sent swinging. The boy sounded quite friendly though.

'Oh, er, just checking where all the Wendy News papers have to go. I'm starting there on Monday.'

'Good for you. What's the pay like?'

'OK.' He'd better not tell him that he'd never even asked. It didn't sound very business-like.

'I wouldn't fancy it, having to get up in the dark every morning.'

'But you *are* up,' Frank pointed out.

'Well, I know. No choice, I've got TB,' and he grinned.

'What's that then?'

'Tiny bladder.'

Frank couldn't think what else to say but he didn't really want to go yet. He kept himself to himself at school because he didn't like people asking too many questions about him, Slob and Dad. They might think the home life of the Tanners was a bit peculiar, and they'd be right. This boy seemed to want to talk though.

Then someone yelled down the stairs. 'Tim? Was that you in the lavatory by any chance?'

'Yes. Sorry, Moira, but I was desperate.' *My mother*, he mouthed at Frank through the gently rocking fern fronds.

'Tim, you do this to me every single morning. And I've told you, once I'm awake, I'm awake. It's really very thoughtless.'

Tim flushed and raised his eyes to heaven.

'I'll go then,' Frank said hurriedly, 'see you Monday,'

26

and he crept back along the immaculate drive, clambered on to his bike and rode off thoughtfully. He'd not liked that voice, it was hectoring and hard, and how daft to tell someone off for doing a pee. If you had to go, you had to go. What was Tim Manning-Sanders supposed to do about his tiny bladder? If it got his mother Moira so uptight, couldn't she pay for an operation? They were obviously loaded with cash.

Fancy the new boy living in a house like that! But why didn't he go to Bryces'? Frank might ask him on Monday, if he was still friendly. And fancy them living next door to the gnomes!

There was obviously something funny going on at the SLG house though. A second old man had joined the first on the doorstep, and they were waving bottles about and singing in cracked, wavering voices.

Near the bottom of the road he saw a man staring up at one of the wedding-cake houses, a smallish neat man with red hair a bit like Tim's. He jumped slightly as Frank pedalled past, moved up on to the pavement and gave him a quick glance. Their eyes met for a second as Frank slowed down for the corner. The man had a dark red birthmark on his neck, spreading out above his collar and under his chin, just as if someone had painted it there.

As he negotiated the dual carriageway, already noisy with its early-morning commuters, Frank thought about Shelley Grant, that very clever girl in the fourth year. She had a birthmark too, not as big as the man's but on her face. You couldn't help looking at it sometimes. It was called a 'port wine stain', Dad said. Doctors could remove them sometimes, when you were little, but Shelley had still got hers, like the man. Frank felt sorry for people with things like that.

As he rode home the face kept floating into his mind; a narrow thin face with bony cheeks that fell in slightly and deep-set, rather mournful eyes. He could remember it because he thought he'd seen it before, in a paper

27

perhaps. Or he could have just noticed the man round Darnley. It wasn't a big town.

So what was he doing in Palace Road so early? There'd not been a builder's van around, or a milk-float, and he'd certainly not been delivering newspapers. For some reason that he couldn't quite put his finger on, Frank felt slightly suspicious. He'd had a furtive look about him somehow, that man with the foxy red hair and the mark on his neck. Had he been sussing out the big houses early in the morning, when all was quiet? He could be a cat burglar. There were break-ins all the time in Denning.

The man with the birthmark. Frank wouldn't forget him in a hurry. He didn't have much of a memory for school-work but he never forgot faces.

Chapter Three

'How's the paper round going then?'

Frank hadn't been going to speak to Tim; he'd decided they couldn't really be friends, him living in a two-up, two-down in Bailey Street and the Manning-Sanderses in that great big house on Palace Road. But the new boy had come straight over to him at mid-morning break, just as friendly as on Saturday morning. He didn't look right at Darnley Comprehensive in his dark grey flannels and herring-bone jacket. There wasn't a uniform at the Comp and most people went round in jeans and sweat-shirts. Tim was going to get picked on before too long, going round dressed like a sixth former at Bryces'. Perhaps Frank should warn him.

He said warily, 'Oh, it's OK.' It wasn't though; size 20 Lily wasn't playing fair with him. She'd not rung to say no so he'd turned up this morning at six-thirty sharp, only to be told he wasn't needed till Wednesday. He was doing the *Spotlight* then apparently, and 'the spare weeklies'.

'Moira thinks a paper round would be a good thing for me as well,' Tim said rather nervously. He was a limp sort of individual; it was the pale, speckled face and the big gap between his neck and his shirt collar.

'Why d'you call your mum Moira?'

'She wants us to, she says "Mum" makes her feel old.'

29

Cass has always called her Moira anyhow, even when she was little.'

'Who's Cass?'

'My sister, she's over there.'

He waved and a girl came across the playground. Oh yes, *Cassie Manning-Sanders*. It was that girl who'd played the violin in last Friday's assembly, when Lord Dewsbury came to talk about his 'bequest'. There was going to be a school competition with big prizes, and Frank already had an idea for it, now he'd got his paper round.

He could see the resemblance between the sister and brother; pale freckly skin, blue eyes, small elfish face. But while Tim's hair was light carrot, Cassie's was crinkly and darker, more the colour of copper-beech leaves, and it hung in great swathes over her shoulders and fell down her back. She was beautiful and she'd been beautiful playing her violin too, even though Mrs Moggridge had spoiled it a bit, thumping too hard on the piano. The sound of that violin had made Frank go all tingly inside and here was its owner, Cass of the golden fingers.

'Aren't you in 4E?' he said, overawed. The E forms were only for really clever people like Shelley Grant, the girl with the birthmark, people who were doing their GCSEs early, 'Express'.

'Suppose I am,' Cass said carelessly. Then, 'Are you our new paper boy?'

'Yes.'

'Well, don't drop my *Smash Hits* down the drain. See you,' and she grinned and walked off. Frank felt a bit dazed. 4E, the class for the shining ones. Cassie, who played Bach on her violin and read *Smash Hits*. All that gorgeous hair as well.

'What's Cass mean?' he said. It sounded so peculiar.

Tim flushed. 'Oh, *Cassandra*. It was Moira's idea. It's Greek. My dad's called Jack, he works in a bank. We're the normal ones, in fact. I'm thick, according to Moira.'

30

'But you got 80 in that maths test,' Frank said. 'That's not *thick*.' He'd come near the bottom; he just couldn't do maths.

'No, but I didn't come top, did I? Moira likes us to come top in everything. It's Cassie's fault. She does. That's the trouble having a sister like her.'

Frank didn't say anything else. He'd always wanted a sister. The only female in their house was Flump 1, except when Lesley came round.

At dinner time Tim was hovering near him again, but he got away and slipped off to the school library. He'd been thinking about Cass Manning-Sanders most of the morning.

'What have you come for, Tanner?' Arthur Parker was on duty, the maths teacher who thought he was a cretin. As Frank came through the door he'd swept his arms round the pile of books he was marking, as if the boy was planning to run off with them and tear them up into bog paper, page by page.

'I want to look something up, on the Greeks,' and he gave Arthur one of his stares. He'd got as much right to use the library as anyone else, and on Mondays the second years were allowed in anyhow. It was their special day.

'What for?'

'A project.' (Projects got you anything in this school, you could get away with murder in the name of doing a project.)

'Oh. Over there then, second shelf down. There's loads of stuff. Hands clean are they, Tanner?'

Frank resisted the temptation to spit in his eye, turned his hands palm side up and thrust them under Arthur Parker's nose. Yes, they *were* clean, he was a clean person. It didn't follow that you were dirty just because you lived in a little house in Bailey Street and had Slob for a brother. He had a bath twice a week and a strip-wash every day. Why else had Wendy News taken him on if he didn't look respectable? The things he could control,

31

Frank took great pains with. It wasn't his fault if he couldn't do maths. Lots of people couldn't.

He soon found Cassandra in a handbook to Greek mythology. She was the daughter of King Priam and Queen Hecuba and the main thing about her was that she could see into the future. Frank had always disliked that sort of thing; Gran Corcoran worked out deaths from tea-leaves and it gave him the creeps. It was worse than just seeing into the future though, as far as the real Cassandra was concerned; in fact, it was terrible. When she made these predictions nobody ever believed her. *Yet they always came true.*

He walked past Arthur Parker and into the corridor, thinking dreamily about Cass and that copper-beech hair. Knowing what might happen in the future was an awful thought, to him. He didn't want to know. He'd got a sneaking feeling that his was looking hopeless and achieveless, like Dad's. Still, he'd landed the job with Wendy News. That was something.

As he was getting on his bike at four o'clock, Tim came up. 'Do you want to come over?' he said. His white china cheeks had pinked slightly and he sounded a bit embarrassed.

'What, now?' Nobody had ever asked Frank back after school before, not at the Comp anyhow. All that had ended years ago, along with birthday parties and jelly.

'Why not? Moira won't be there,' he added. 'She's lecturing this afternoon, she teaches at the Poly.' The absence of Moira was obviously meant to be an added inducement. Tim Manning-Sanders clearly didn't like his mother very much.

'Well, OK then.' This quiet boy with carroty hair wasn't exactly Personality of the Year, but Frank was quite curious to see the house. He could find out about next-door's gnomes too, and Cassie might be there. 'I'll have to phone my dad first,' he said.

'Your dad? Why?'

32

'Well, he's at home this afternoon and he'll worry if I don't show up.' That was putting it mildly. If Frank was five minutes late Dad was out on Bailey Street, looking for him; ten minutes late and he'd constructed a whole scenario in which he'd been flattened by a corporation bus, or else abducted by the Larkfield Killer. What he needed was something special to love and worry about. The Flumps, Frank and Malcolm obviously weren't enough.

The payphone outside the school gate was free and Frank dialled, trying to breathe shallowly. Someone had peed in the kiosk.

He wondered once again why the Manning-Sanders parents had sent Cassie and Tim to this dump. People didn't pee in phone-boxes at Bryces'.

Dad sounded pleased about the invitation. 'That's lovely, son,' he said warmly. 'You'll have room for a bit of supper though, won't you? Your Gran left a pie.'

Oh, Gawd. Gran's pies were like those fruit-cakes in the telly commercial, so heavy they almost made a hole in the table. He always got chronic indigestion after one of Gran Corcoran's pies.

'I'll try,' he said, secretly determined to eat everything he was offered at Tim's so as to leave no possible room for the steak and kidney bomb. 'Anyhow, you OK? You sound brighter.' Dad had been very depressed recently.

'I'm fine, son. I've written to the bank again and asked Mr Brocklehurst to get on with my application. I've said I want a reply by return of post. I'm right, aren't I?'

'Course you are. See you later then.'

Frank hung up and went back to the bike racks. *Dad and the bank.* Sometimes he wondered who was looking after whom.

Cass had obviously got home first because Frank noticed a girl's bike propped against the double garage, and in the hall, on a curly coat-stand, he saw the dark navy

33

jacket and pink scarf she'd been wearing in the playground. Cass Manning-Sanders had style.

'Let's go down to my room,' Tim said, 'unless you want something to eat first?'

'No, I'm OK . . . Is that your Cass playing?' Down the staircase floated the sound of a solo violin, a sadsweet, long-ago sound that sent a funny shiver down Frank's back.

'Yes. She's got an exam next week so she's got to do a lot of extra practising.'

'Sounds brilliant.'

'She is,' Tim said gloomily. 'It's sickening. Take a pew.'

He pulled a heap of clothes off the big leather armchair and Frank sat down, looking round with interest. The room was much bigger than he'd thought on Saturday and everything was new and bang up to date. The furniture was the kind they sold at Habitat, in Manchester, and all the colours matched. Dark green for the carpet, pale green for the walls and a single picture over the bed, nothing you could recognize, just huge swirly lines, all the greens you'd ever seen.

The bedding was green too, with jazzy black patterns, but Tim had obviously gone off to school without straightening it. Before he could screw it up Frank had read the note pinned to the pillowcase: 'Make this bed and tidy this room. M.'

In a corner he saw what looked like a TV set but it was draped in a green cloth with only the chrome stand showing. Another note, in the same thick black print as the one on the bed, announced: 'This device carries a government health warning.'

'What's that mean? And why's the telly covered up?'

Tim went that pale pink colour again. It was a pity he blushed so easily, it clashed with his hair. 'Well, my mother thinks I watch too much TV, when I ought to be doing my homework.'

'But we hardly ever get homework.'

'I know, that's one of the things she's got against the school. She says she's going to write and complain. I'm dreading it.'

'Why don't you go to Bryces'?' Frank said, 'and your sister could have gone to St Monica's. They're good schools, they are, everyone says so.' Then he added casually, 'My dad wanted me to go to Bryces', as a matter of fact.'

'So why didn't you?'

'Not got the cash, have we? Why didn't you?'

'Oh, the usual story in our house. My father was all for it, got the forms and everything, but Moira put her foot down, said they weren't paying ridiculous fees when they already paid a load of tax and that we'd be better off at the Comprehensive with everyone else. She'd been told it was a good school but she says she's not so sure, now. Anyhow, she won, as usual, so we both ended up at the Comp.'

Won. He made it sound like guerrilla warfare. One thing about not having two parents, at least you didn't get caught in the crossfire. People at school were always going on about their mums and dads arguing, and knocking each other about. Why did anyone ever get married at all? That's what Frank had always wondered.

'Did you say your father worked in a bank?' He sounded a bit downtrodden, Tim's father did. Perhaps he was only an upmarket version of Dad.

'Yes. He's just had a big promotion, that's why we've moved here. He's managing the Moseley Street branch in Manchester now; he commutes.'

'Which bank?'

'Friendly Northern. You know, "We're the little one so we try harder." He helped with that advertising campaign on TV.'

Frank felt a bit odd when he heard it was the Northern; this boy's dad was obviously quite an influential person. That slogan he'd helped with had been on telly and everything. If they were difficult about Dad's loan perhaps Mr Manning-Sanders could help.

'My father banks with them,' he said. 'Banks' sounded impressive but the truth was rather different. Dad didn't have much more than three hundred pounds in the whole world. Frank knew because he'd looked in the deposit books. His money was in four or five different places, a bit with the Leeds, a bit with the Halifax and a bit in the Post Office. He said it was 'safer' that way, just in case one of them went bust. And his Northern account wasn't in a big branch, all marble and rubber plants like the one Tim's father obviously worked in. It was on the corner of Shorrock Street, a little shack that looked like some public conveniences.

'I wouldn't mind working in a bank,' Tim said. 'My mother says it's boring though.'

'But your *dad* works in one,' Frank pointed out, not really understanding.

'I know. She says he's boring too, and that one bore's enough in the family.'

Moira, the writer of cryptic notes in thick felt tip, the woman who covered the telly up as if it was a parrot. Frank hadn't actually met her yet but he felt he was going to want to kill her on sight. This was a gorgeous house and everything, but the Manning-Sanders family didn't sound a bit happy. There was more love and contentment at their place, even with Malcolm around, because Dad cared about them so much, and showed it.

'What do you want to do then, when you've left school?' Tim said. He clearly wanted to get off the subject of his parents.

'Dunno. I quite like fiddling with electrical things. My father's in the electrical business. Actually, he's applied for one of those loans, to expand. I like your bedroom,' he went on hurriedly, rather wishing he'd not mentioned the loan, in case Tim asked awkward questions. 'I'm having a new room soon, in our basement probably.' 'Basement' sounded better than 'cellar' and that

36

was where he'd end up, unless Slob actually did move out.

'Cass helped me with this,' Tim said. 'Moira told us how much we could spend and we chose the colours and everything. It didn't really cost much.'

'It *looks* expensive,' Frank said. 'It's brilliant.'

'We could help you with yours, if you like,' Tim said shyly. 'Can I come round and see it?'

'Er, well, it's got this damp problem at the moment,' Frank told him. 'But when that's sorted out you can.' Though he couldn't really imagine what the Manning-Sanderses would think of 14 Bailey Street. His plans for a room were just dreams really. But you had to *have* dreams.

Over their heads they heard feet scrunching suddenly on gravel, a key turn in a lock and a front door being opened then slammed shut.

'It's Moira,' Tim whispered, looking round a bit wildly, kicking his school case under a chair and pulling the bed straight. 'They must have cancelled her afternoon lecture.'

His nervousness was catching; Frank gulped and looked round for an escape route. There were two doors off the bedroom. One led to a little bathroom, the other upstairs to Moira, who sounded as if she was ripping the day's post open.

'Oh, *God*,' they heard, 'that's *ridiculous*! Cassie, come down here, will you? And where's Tim? This phone bill's absolutely *phenomenal*. From now on you will both write down *all calls*. Otherwise we'll just have to manage *without* a telephone. Cassie . . . *Tim!*'

The violin stopped abruptly and someone came clumping down the stairs. Slowly, pulling an agonized face, Tim went towards the door. Frank followed reluctantly, looking his last on the fabulous green bedroom which, as the afternoon light faded, was beginning to resemble some vast aquarium with white-faced Tim

37

flipping about it mournfully, with that down-in-the-mouth fish expression.

'Moira, this is Frank Tanner. He's in my class. Frank, this is my mother.'

Frank was tall for his age but Mrs Manning-Sanders still looked down on him. She must be nearly six foot and she was very square about the shoulders, as if they'd forgotten to take the hanger out at the dry-cleaner's.

'How do you do, Frank?' Her voice was posh; it made him feel very low-grade, very Lancashire. And the eyes on him, though brown, were cool and fault-finding. All of a sudden, he wanted to go home. 'Oh, I'm OK thanks. Great. Er, I was just leaving actually. I've – I've got homework.'

They had too. Miss Halliwell, their form teacher, had set them an English project. They were supposed to start 'making notes' tonight, about Lord Dewsbury's competition. Frank was quite keen to do it, for once. He'd got this good idea brewing.

'Well, *that*'s a turn-up for the books.'

'What?'

'Homework. According to Tim you very rarely get any. Things are obviously looking up.' She didn't really mean it, though, she was obviously being sarcastic. Frank hated that.

'See you then, Tim,' and he walked to the front door.

Mrs Manning-Sanders opened it. 'You must come to tea,' she said. 'Come on Thursday, it's my early day.'

'All right, I will. Thanks very much.'

'See you, Frank.' That was Cassie standing under the curly coat-rack, looking as if she'd floated down those deep-carpeted stairs on invisible wings. Her copper hair was one glorious cloud round her face.

He pedalled off straight away, not stopping until he'd put half a dozen houses between himself and the Manning-Sanderses. Then he braked and stood under a street light, to inspect what he'd slipped in his pocket just before following Tim up the stairs. It was a snap of Cass in a blue sun-dress, standing in the doorway of an ancient church. There'd been three photos, almost identical, on a table in Tim's room, so he'd never miss this one. And Frank would give it back anyhow, when he'd had a little look at it.

You couldn't call it stealing.

Chapter Four

On the Wednesday Frank was awake by five. It was his big day, the day he was going to be a newsboy proper, provided Wedding Dress Wendy didn't break her promise. He didn't want to be late.

He was all set to go out by half past; then he realized that he'd left his anorak upstairs so he crept back to get it. Slob was lying flat on his back, snoring with his great big mouth open. His thick hairy torso was naked except for some fancy boxer shorts. This pair had brown bears on, cuddling half-way up a palm tree. They looked a lot prettier than him and Lesley, nibbling at each other under the street light when they said goodnight.

On his way down again he peeped into the back bedroom. Dad always slept with his door open and the landing light on 'in case they needed him in the small hours'. Frank tiptoed across the carpet and stared down at the neat little hump under the blankets. He could only see a bit of polished head with its Horlicks blodges and one little hand clutching the edge of the sheet, in case someone came and ripped it away in the night.

Then his eyes wandered to the bedside table. Under the *Flatten Your Stomach!* book there was a cutting from the *Spotlight*. He slid it out carefully and took it across to the door so that he could read it.

It said '*Denning Spotlight* Lonelyhearts Club – Does Shyness Hold You Back? Put a message in print and make friends the easy way.' On the left were rows and rows of little advertisements. 'Knight in shining armour (47) seeks tin-opener (same age)' . . . 'Bubbly blonde, with most tremendous tan, seeks friendship with non-smoking, attractive gentleman in his thirties' . . . 'Attractive guy (39) would like to meet super lady for jolly evenings out. Photo appreciated.' There were dozens of the things.

At the edge of the column in red biro Dad had obviously been drafting an ad of his own. 'Quiet lonely chap, 45, would like to meet sincere lady for lasting relationship. House owner, two sons.'

Frank carefully replaced the cutting underneath the stomach book and the tears pricked his eyes. It wasn't the ad itself that bothered him. If you were determined to get married then doing it this way seemed quite a good idea to him, slowly, one step at a time. It was the 'two sons', the idea that Dad wouldn't marry anyone who didn't want them as well. It was real love, that was.

Before going downstairs again he bent down and kissed the bit of shiny head. He didn't care if Malcolm did say he was 'queer'. What was the point of loving somebody if you never showed it? He wanted to do well at things for Dad's sake, as well as his own. Winning this Lord Dewsbury competition would be great and he'd made a good start last night. You had to do a project on 'Our Town', and Frank had decided to base his on local newspapers. It was the perfect topic for a delivery boy. He brought his bike round from the shed and set off towards Denning. Their road looked really odd without its cars. Last week the police had had double yellow lines painted right along it because it was getting so busy. There was only one now, on the whole of Bailey Street, an old Renault 4 parked outside their house. Sellotaped to the windscreen was a fifteen-pounds parking ticket.

Frank shivered slightly as he pedalled past. Malcolm

was going to love that. There'd be a row with the traffic wardens, he could see it coming.

On his way through the Larkfield Estate something uncanny happened. He was going quite fast, anxious to turn up on the dot of half past six, when he rounded a corner into the steep long bit and hit somebody. He saw it coming, rammed his brakes on and put his foot to the ground, but it was too late. The man, who'd been peering into an old Morris Minor parked outside one of the houses, had jerked back when he heard the bike and gone straight into the front wheel.

'I'm sorry,' Frank said, letting go of the handlebars and running over to him. The man in the road was rubbing at his shin and already scrambling to his feet. 'Sorry, but I didn't see you. You OK?'

'Yeah, yeah, sure. I'm all right.'

When Frank got a proper look at him, he did a double take. It was the man he'd seen in Palace Road, the red-haired man, the man with the birthmark. The odd thing was that he didn't swear at him or anything, he didn't even make a mild complaint. Most people would have done more than that, and somebody like Slob may well have thumped him. This bloke, white-faced and thin with rather bulgy eyes, seemed to want to get away as quickly as possible. Had he recognized Frank, from the other morning?

He didn't actually look as if he came off Larkfield, he was rather too clean and tidy. Navy anorak, black jeans, black suede shoes, quite new-looking. Suede was 'in' this year, according to Slob. The man was older than him, though, thirty at least. Frank stared at him as he brushed himself down, not quite knowing what to say.

He was mumbling 'sorry' when the man walked off. After he'd disappeared round the corner he peered through the window of the Morris Minor. Lying on the back seat was a shiny black 'executive' brief-case, the sort he planned to buy himself for school, when he'd saved up some paper money.

Then, as he bent down to retrieve his bike, he trod on something that went right through the sole of his left shoe, digging into his foot. *Ouch.* When he got it out he saw that it was a piece of sharp wire, probably a bit of a coathanger.

Interesting. You could use wire to get into cars, he'd seen that packs of times on the telly. Was that what Foxy was up to then, creeping about so early in the morning when nobody but the paper boys had a right to be up and doing?

In his pocket Frank found a big man's handkerchief, ironed and put there by Dad, no doubt, to impress Wedding Dress Wendy. He wrapped it carefully round the bit of wire and zipped it into his anorak pocket. One of these days the man with the birthmark might turn up again.

As he pedalled towards Wendy News, he thought again about his 'Our Town' project. Perhaps he should concentrate on crime. There was plenty of it about and it would make much more interesting reading than rose queens and old people's coach trips to North Wales. They weren't news items at all. That mysterious-looking foxy individual had certainly got him thinking.

This time when he got to the shop, Lily was ready for him. 'You're late,' she said, pointing behind her to the clock on the wall. He was too, five whole minutes. It was that brush with Foxy. And after waking up at five o'clock.

'Sorry,' he muttered. 'I came off my bike.'

'Bryces' boys have been here since six-twenty,' she said moodily, 'and they have a longer day than you. Don't get home from school till seven at night, some of them.'

No, they wouldn't, Frank said to himself. It was all that swotting they had to do for their EEGs.

'Well, I'm all set now,' he said cheerfully, pushing Dad's glasses back up his nose and trying to resemble a bright boy. (The minute he was out of sight those specs

43

were going into his pocket. Percy's printout was all swimmy with them on.)

'Here you are then.' After the printout came a luminous, plastic sack on a broad canvas strap with the word *Spotlight* emblazoned across it in banana yellow. 'Every house on the list gets one, Wednesdays and Saturdays. The extras are on it as well.'

She pulled a fag from behind her ear and lit up but Frank didn't budge. It was high time he asked about his pay, how many hours he was doing and whether this was a regular job. He said, 'What are you paying me?' but those little piggies had made him very nervous and his voice was a squeak.

'Still got to sort that out with Mr Chadwick,' she said evasively. Then, more aggressive and blowing smoke in his face, 'Look, do you want this job or don't you?'

'Yes, yes I do, I'm just going,' and he was through the door in two seconds flat and off up the road with what felt like half a hundredweight of *Denning Spotlights*.

Wedding Dress Wendy knew what she was doing all right, taking Frank Tanner on, Frank Tanner the lanky lad from Bailey Street who'd obviously do anything for a job. She'd given him the longest round of the lot and it was going to take him hours. Good job it was nothing important at school today, only 'musical appreciation' with piano-bashing Mrs Moggridge and he nearly always skipped that anyhow.

He'd never really thought seriously about front doors till he started pushing *Spotlights* through them. Now he did, and of what they told you about people. That's probably why it all took such a long time, it was so interesting, and definitely something to go in his project.

For a start, some were filthy dirty, even here in up-market Denning. There was nothing to compare with the gleaming red front door in Bailey Street that Dad wiped down with Flash every single Saturday morning. One front-door step was covered with milk bottles, dozens of them, all smeary-looking and cobwebby. Surely nobody delivered milk here any more? The people inside must be dead.

Still, fat Lily had said 'Every *single* address on the list' and that the *Spotlight* people'd check up. So he shoved one through obediently, hearing it flap spookily into what was obviously an empty house. If they weren't quite dead, the *Spotlight* might come in useful anyhow; this issue had a big ad on the back page for Braithwaite's Complete Funeral Service – 'Quick and Efficient Service Guaranteed for Your Loved Ones.'

One house, in Victoria Avenue, he christened the No Anything house. 'No leaflets, no hawkers, no free newspapers' said the typed label stuck to the letter-box. Well, the *Spotlight* was free but he'd got his orders, so he shoved one through hastily and ran off.

Not fast enough though. A huge woman with a bust the size of the Continental Shelf suddenly materialized on the doorstep as he swung his leg over his crossbar. 'Excuse *me*,' she shouted. 'Can't you read? *No free papers*,' and she waved the *Spotlight* at him.

'Not today,' he shouted back, but silently, pedalling off. Anyhow, she should be grateful to him. The *Spotlight* carried regular announcements about Weight Watchers meetings, and it did a good line in outsize wedding dresses too.

One house, near the end, he just refused to go into. It had a six-foot fence all round it and barbed wire on top of that. The minute he rattled the gate there were ferocious barking noises from all sides. It sounded like a pack of highly trained sniffer dogs, all psyching themselves up to pounce and tear him to pieces.

But Lily had said *every* house, so he tossed a paper over the fence and made off. There was an uncanny silence afterwards. Did the *Spotlight* taste of Chum or were the dogs all reading the comic strips on page eleven? They weren't very funny, not nearly as good as *Mad* magazine, which he'd skipped through rather furtively outside 17 Henley Drive before popping it through with a *Spotlight*. *Mad* did well in Denning. Tim got it too.

Seven forty-five and he'd finished, all except for the Manning-Sanderses and the S L G house. He'd kept those till the very end; they were his treats.

He was saved the job of pushing the *Spotlight* through 103, because two people came puffing up to him just as he was walking along the drive.

'We've already had our paper this morning,' a familiar voice said, rather snappishly. 'Your shop doesn't deliver to us. Oh, it's *you*.' Tim's mother was looming over him in a shocking-pink track suit. Her face was all red and sweaty and she'd obviously been out for her morning jog.

'It's – it's not the usual round,' Frank stammered, peering up past the heaving pink bosom into the cool brown eyes. 'It's the *Spotlight* this is, it's new. Here –' and he shoved it at her, 'it doesn't cost anything.'

'Well, I'm not at all sure we want it,' she said, glancing suspiciously at the main headline ('Darnley Cemeteries Face Big Squeeze'). 'It's just another bit of junk to go in the rubbish as far as I'm concerned.'

'Not necessarily, dear. We'll certainly have it,' and the small man at her side put his hand out and took it. 'Mmm, they take a lot of local advertising. Could be useful.'

'You're Tim's friend, aren't you?' he said. Mr Manning-Sanders was just as Frank had imagined, another little dad, but the thin and wiry type, the sort that went climbing mountains. What remained of his hair was sandy-pink, the colour that had come out in Tim as carrots and in Cassie as autumn leaves.

'Yes, we're in the same class.'

'That's nice. Our Tim's always been a bit of a loner, the shy sort. Keep on going with your paper round, it's a good discipline, that is.'

'I've told Tim to apply for one,' sniffed Moira, 'but

46

he'll never get his act together. I hope he's doing his practising.'

Practising . . . before *breakfast*? 'What on?' said Frank faintly.

'The piano. Only Grade 1. Mind you, we've all got music in us, as I never cease telling him.'

Through the window, as if on cue, came the sound of a scale being thumped up and down, jerkily, as if the person really hated it. Poor Tim. Frank felt really sorry for him.

'Anyway, we're seeing you tomorrow, aren't we?'

'Oh. Are you?'

'Yes. You're coming home after school with Tim. It's my early day.'

'Oh, OK. Well, er, thanks very much.'

'You could come in for some breakfast now,' the dad said kindly. 'You must have been up for hours.'

'No, it's all right. I've not quite finished actually. See you.'

He really didn't fancy breakfast with the Manning-Sanderses; Moira clearly wasn't a morning person at all.

Since Saturday, next-door's gnomes had obviously started a clean-up operation. The skip in the road was now piled high with bottles and cans, and on top they'd dumped the 'For Sale' notice. Someone had been sweeping leaves up too; there was a big pile of them outside the front door.

It was wide open and Frank didn't know what to do with the *Spotlight*. Should he go in and leave it by the phone or ought he just to chuck it on the mat? There were probably 'laws' about paper boys crossing thresholds, laws which Wedding Dress Wendy could use to give him the push. She didn't really want him doing her papers, he'd decided, she was too unfriendly. She'd probably only agreed because she'd once known Dad.

He was standing there thinking about it when somebody tapped him on the shoulder. 'Goodo,' a voice said, tweaking the *Spotlight* from between his fingers. 'This'll be just the place to pick up a bit of furniture for my old men. Does it come out every week?'

If she was of the gnome species then she was obviously a leprechaun, because she had a very soft, very Irish voice. It reminded him of Gran Tanner, who'd died when he was little. 'Liverpool–Irish' she'd been, that's why Dad was called Feargus.

'Twice,' he said, 'there'll be another one on Saturday. Here, have two, they gave me a few extras.'

The leprechaun was already scanning the small ads. ' "Axminster Carpet, dark red, 9 feet by 12 feet" . . .mm . . . that might do. I'll have to measure the room.'

Peeping past her, Frank could see the pegs with the purple macs on. Only five now, though, two of the gnomes must have gone off early to the mines. This woman was all purple too, purple skirt, purple cardigan, pale purple blouse. Even her tights were purple, quite trendy. It was the hair that gave him the clue, or rather, the lack of hair. If she'd got any at all it was pulled right back and hidden under a tight white band, a bit like a vicar's dog-collar. From the band came a purple head-dress, like a nurse's, falling down in folds and covering her neck. She was a nun.

Frank stared. 'Are you bald?' he blurted out, then he felt himself going red. He'd never meant to *say* it, it was just what he'd wondered in his mind. It must be getting up so early, without any breakfast; it had obviously made him light-headed.

'Not quite,' she said, and she laughed, rather a dirty laugh it sounded too, not filthy-dirty, like when Slob laughed, but, well, *human*. Frank was intrigued because he knew a little bit about nuns. Gran Tanner's sister Bessie had been one and Dad used to visit her some-times, when he was little. He'd told Frank how they had to talk to her through an iron grille, and how she never came out of the nunnery but prayed all the time.

So he'd always wondered about nuns, having had one in the family, what they had to eat and whether they went to the lavatory. You couldn't really imagine it. Here was a real live one within spitting distance and she was unpinning the nurse-hat thing and shaking out long fair hair.

'There you are, I've got plenty. Only we have to keep it tucked up, it's the *rule*,' and quick as a flash she'd bundled it all up again and fixed the purple material in place with two big grips.

He said, slightly embarrassed now, 'Well, here's your extra *Spotlight*, oh, and the *TV Times* – but it's not for you, is it?' But it said SLG quite clearly on the top.

'Yes, it's ours. It came very late last week. Sister Geraldine was cross.'

'Is she the boss then?'

'Sort of. We don't really have "bosses", we all muck in. There are only six of us here at the moment.'

'So what's your name then?'

By now he'd followed her into the hall. Next to the old black telephone there was a little bowl of white flowers and on the wall above them a painting of the Virgin Mary holding the baby Jesus. They both looked very overweight.

'Maggie.'

'Is that all?'

'Yes, that's my name. Why?'

'I – well, it doesn't sound very . . .'

'Nun-like?'

'No.'

'It's actually Sister Mary Magdalen, if you want the whole works, only please don't call me that.'

Mary Magdalen. Now he actually knew about her, but only because of his RE lessons. She was . . . he racked his brains . . . some kind of bad woman, wasn't she?

'Have you heard of her?' Maggie asked him, fiddling with the white flowers and crossing herself as her eyes met those of the fat Virgin Mary in the painting.

'Yes, we've done her at school.'

'She was a prostitute. If she'd been around today, I think they'd have made her join a trade union,' and she gave him a shy smile.

She was really very pretty, in a clean, scrubbed sort of way, the healthy, brown-bread type you could see striding across Darnley Moor. What a funny thing to say, though, about Mary Magdalen joining a union!

'So why've you got that name then?' he said curiously.

'I chose it, when I was admitted to the Order.'

'But why?'

'Because Our Lord loved her, very much,' and she fingered a plain gold ring on her wedding finger.

Frank stared at it. 'Were you married then, before you joined up?' She looked much too young.

'No. We wear a ring because we've given ourselves to Our Lord. It's just a symbol.'

Frank looked down at her hands. They didn't go with the rest of her, they were too worn, too old-looking, and there were yellow paint stains all over them. She saw him looking and put them behind her back. 'We've been painting the day room,' she explained, 'and I can't get it all off.'

'You need white spirit for that. I could bring you some.'

'Well, that's very kind, all offers gratefully received in this place. Er, do you want some breakfast? I've just brewed up for Eric.'

Frank hesitated. It was nearly eight o'clock and he ought to slip home. But what the heck, he could always ring Dad from the phone-box outside school. He rather wanted to meet 'Eric', and find out why nuns took the *TV Times*. It'd be something else to go in his newspaper project.

'OK,' he said, dumping his fluorescent *Spotlight* bag at the feet of the Virgin and following Maggie down the cool hall.

The day room was big and empty except for a couple

of very tatty armchairs and a television set. Huddled up, watching *Breakfast Time*, was the ugly old man with the lip he'd seen on Saturday morning, sitting on the doorstep. The main smell in the room was new paint, yellow walls, yellow windows, yellow door. Maggie had obviously gone mad with Sunflower gloss and emulsion; there were tins of it in one corner. But there was an under-smell too, that of somebody who never had a bath, a smell so strong that it tugged at Frank's empty stomach. So he kept his distance.

Maggie marched right up to him though, and put her hand on his. 'Want a cup of tea, Eric? Fancy a few flakes?'

Eric scowled, stuck his great lip out and concentrated on the TV screen, where a woman in a bright green leotard was busy doing healthful early-morning exercises, showing you how to deal with the flabby upper arm. Dad was probably watching it too, with the Flumps.

'Do you want a cup of *tea*, Eric?'

No response.

'Well, if you do, come along to the kitchen. I've just brewed up.'

'He's grumpy because I've taken his whisky away,' she whispered. 'Look, this boy's – what's your name?'

'Frank.'

'Look, Frank's brought you the new *TV Times*. They're having a party on *Coronation Street* next Monday. Now, you'll like that, Eric.'

Still no reply but, as they went back into the hall, he thought he heard 'Bloody woman' and a loud belch. It felt quite like home here; it could have been Slob.

'I didn't know this was a nunnery,' Frank said, chewing cornflakes at a big scrubbed table (they seemed mad on scrubbing in this place). 'What's SLG stand for then?'

'Ah, ha. You tell me.' When she smiled her whole face lit up.

'Dunno.' Well, he couldn't very well say Society for Lost Gnomes.

'Sisters of the Love of God. We've only been here two weeks. Someone left us this house in a will; it's in a terrible state.'

'Looks as if some real weirdos have been in it, if you ask me,' Frank said, 'all those bottles.'

'You're right. There were squatters here for months, we had to get the police. Want some toast?'

'Thanks. What about that old man?' munched Frank. 'I saw two of them on Saturday. What were they hanging about for?'

'Well, I guess they're the kind of leftovers, from when the house was empty and people slept rough in it. I don't mind them, just so long as they don't bring their drink in.'

'But why come to you, I mean, *nuns*?'

Maggie shrugged. 'I suppose they know we won't turn them away. Sister Geraldine says we mustn't. They can have cups of tea, and sandwiches, but we can't give them any money. If we did it would just go straight down their throats. Eric's not very well, you know, he shouldn't drink whisky. We don't really need that great big sitting-room so we're doing it up for them. Someone gave us the TV last week, and someone else gave us the paint.'

'Don't you have telly then?'

'No, not for ourselves. I had it at home but I never liked it much. It was such a small house and there were seven children. I could never get away from it.'

'I can't either,' Frank said with feeling, and he found himself telling her all his troubles, how much he hated sharing with Slob and his secret plans to move into the cellar, about Dad's advert for a sincere lady and a lasting relationship, and about the Friendly Northern Bank not replying. He told her all about his plans to go in for Lord Dewsbury's 'Our Town' competition, and how he might win a big prize, to get things for his room. She listened so intently, and with such an interested look on her face, that he nearly mentioned the man with the birthmark

52

too, but he bit it back. He felt Maggie wouldn't like him harbouring nasty suspicions about someone he'd merely seen on the street. She was great, all kindness and warm feeling, like the older sister he'd always dreamed of, and his mother too, a bit.

'All I want's a room of my own,' he concluded, 'it doesn't seem much, does it?'

'It certainly doesn't. I mean, I've got one, and I'm a nun.'

'Yes, but you're not the typical nun, are you?' and Frank looked at her shyly. She was almost as pretty as Cass.

Maggie gave him that smashing smile again. 'Well, what's "typical"? I mean, how many typical nuns do you know?'

After a minute she added, 'I could always say a little prayer.'

'What for?'

'Well, your new room, a nice girlfriend for your dad, things like that.'

'No, don't. My gran says prayers and it gives me the creeps. They don't work anyway, prayers.'

'All right. I won't. Tell me if you change your mind though.'

Before he went off she somehow got him to promise that he'd come back again. She said she'd certainly like to borrow Dad's white spirit and that they needed a proper notice for the front gate. Frank, who had a steady hand, offered to paint her one, if he could get the stuff.

He arrived at school half-way through music appreciation, which seemed to consist of most people appreciating Mrs Moggridge's knickers, revealed as she crossed her plump thighs to sit on the teacher's table. Nobody was listening to the music she'd put on for them, except Tim Manning-Sanders, and he looked half asleep.

Frank crept in at the back, got comfy, and was dozing

53

off himself within about three minutes. A five a.m. start was just too early; he'd have to get better organized.

He had a lovely kip, though, dreaming about Cass and Sister Maggie, both playing violins and writing poetry, and sending him big, flowery cards when he won the Dewsbury Competition. Sweet, sweet dreams.

A bare week ago he'd had no women in his life and no job. Now he was a paper boy with Wendy News and there were two pretty girls taking quite an interest in him.

Things had definitely taken a turn for the better.

Chapter Five

On Thursday 2H's teacher, Miss Halliwell, had the forms about the competition, but they nearly didn't get them because they were in disgrace for Passing the Bin. This was a form of protest, something they only did with really boring teachers, and Miss Halliwell was a boredom specialist. Her RE lessons were guaranteed to put the whole class to sleep. All she ever did was to make them write notes out of textbooks, one between three, which was no good at all for Frank who wrote extremely slowly and always got behind.

What you did was to get the bin from desk to desk without the teacher noticing. Every time it stopped you were supposed to put something horrible in it, then pass it on. 2H were rather good at Passing the Bin; Miss Halliwell had given them a lot of practice.

This time someone put a load of chewing-gum in it, someone else a handful of fingernails which they'd been saving up in a pencil case. Ricky Dobson, who always had colds, blew his nose hard and dropped a really snotty tissue in, then Maxine Fenton, who suffered from 'wax', got a big ball of it out of her left ear and flicked that in too. As the bin moved silently from desk to desk it got more and more disgusting.

Miss Halliwell finally intercepted it between Tim and Frank and she was very hurt. She sent Brian Wilde off to empty it then said, very red in the face and nearly crying, '*Right*, you can jolly well make notes for the rest of the lesson, for all I care,' and sat down. Well, what was new? They did that all the time anyhow.

Ten minutes before the bell went, though, somebody brought a piece of paper from the headmaster, and the forms. Miss Halliwell stood up again and told them all to listen. 'You don't deserve an opportunity like this,' she told them, 'but under the terms of the Dewsbury Bequest which you all heard about last week, someone in this class could win a great deal of money. There are three prizes, junior, middle and senior, and each one is worth a hundred pounds. There are runners-up prizes too.'

'But what for, Miss?' Typical of her not to say what you actually had to *do*.

'The subject is Darnley-in-Makerfield, "Our Town", as you heard last week. Lord Dewsbury was born in Darnley and so was his father, who made this bequest to the school. It says here that the prizes will go to the boys or girls in each section who, in the opinion of the judges, "submit the most interesting and original piece of research on any aspect of life in 'Our Town', past, present or future." '

'What's "research" mean then, Miss?'
'And what does "submit" mean?'
'When do they decide who's won?'
'Will it be a hundred pounds in cash?'

Questions were hailing in from all sides now; they were all interested in money.

'Please be quiet for a minute. In simple terms, it means you do your own personal project on whichever slant you decide to take. The school will supply folders and paper, the rest is up to you. By the way, you've only got a month to do it in. It says here that the results will be announced on the last day of term. I must say, I'd quite like to win one of these prizes myself.'

Poor Miss Halliwell. She had a crushed and crumpled sort of face, and terribly thin hair, scraped right back so that the pink of her scalp showed through. Her flat shoes were plastic, her brown skirt looked as if it had been cobbled together from two old sacks, her brown, home-made cardigan was all lumpy and lopsided. Frank had thought she dressed like that because she was religious, but Sister Maggie was quite smart. Secretly, he felt a bit sorry for Miss Halliwell. They should give her one of the hundred pound prizes for some new clothes.

2H had gone quiet and broody now and they stayed like that till the bell went. The thought of all that money had obviously concentrated the mind. Some people were already scribbling things down in their rough books.

Frank stared out of the window and watched a sparrow in the playground pecking at a bit of orange peel. A hundred pounds would go a long way towards doing up his new cellar bedroom, whereas it'd take weeks to earn money of that order with Wendy News. He'd got a good idea but what real chance did he have? He always got low marks in English because he couldn't spell and it took him so long to do neat handwriting.

Still, nobody else appeared to have thought about local newspapers. At the end of the lesson people seemed to be talking about historical things mainly, the parish church, and the town hall. He was going to keep very quiet about his brainwave till the projects were in, otherwise someone might copy and do a whole lot better.

He couldn't really bring in the man with the birthmark though. He was definitely a bit suspicious-looking but that didn't make him a criminal. All he could do was keep his eyes open. But if he saw him hanging around again, perhaps he'd follow him home, and see what he was up to.

Tea at 103 Palace Road was a bit nerve-racking. For a start Cassie wasn't there; she was having an extra violin lesson, and it was mainly to see Cassie that he'd come. Second, he just couldn't eat the food. Moira didn't eat meat at all and she said that, although she wouldn't *force* them, she was hoping that the rest of the family would copy, eventually. Thursday, she briskly informed him, was always a 'meatless' day at 103. He didn't mind, did he?

Well, he did. He wasn't against people going meatless; it was just that he'd always had a bit of a funny stomach like Dad, and cheese gave him pains. The big wedge of pie she set in front of him seemed to be solid cheese and when he stuck his fork in, it came up with rubber strings stuck to the prongs. He ate all round the wedge carefully, lettuce, tomato, cucumber, cold beans, until the plate was as clean as a whistle. All except for the rubber pie which just sat there, accusing him.

In the end he took a very deep breath and said nervously, 'I'm very sorry Mrs Manning-Sanders but cheese gives me pains.'

His plate was immediately whisked away. 'That's quite all right.' It wasn't really though, he could tell from her tone of voice. Frank preferred people who said what they meant, not funny 'hurt' people like Moira Manning-Sanders, and she always seemed so angry about everything too. He tried really hard to make up, with the pudding, but he didn't like that much either. It was home-made yoghurt with apricots stirred in and it was all gritty and sour. At school Tim had explained that they didn't have sugar in the house, and biscuits were banned, in case they got fillings. The only cake allowed at 103 was one Moira made with carrot in it. Tim said it was nice but Frank hated carrots and he definitely couldn't eat all this yoghurt; he'd never fancied cold slippery things.

While he sat fiddling with it Moira was busy going through Tim's school case. First she unearthed the maths test, then a geography test, then a copy of *Private Eye* with a rude picture of the Queen on the cover. Everything was dumped on the table, with the pie and the yoghurt, and inspected with an eagle eye. She ignored the eighty per cent for maths and concentrated on the geography.

'Mmm. Six out of ten. Really, Tim, you do throw marks away. And look at this, no capital letters, no full stops, messy horrible drawings. You should be ashamed of yourself. I wouldn't have given you one out of ten for work like that. It's no wonder you're in 2H. H for Hopeless.'

'Mum. H is for Halliwell. She's our form teacher.'

Tim, who'd been his usual nervous pinky colour all through tea, now flushed scarlet. But his mother just carried on. It was as if she'd forgotten Frank's actual existence.

'And who gave you this?' she demanded.

The rude *Private Eye* picture showed the Queen's head but the body wore a very skimpy bikini with a lot of bosom dropping out.

Frank wanted to laugh, so he shoved some gritty yoghurt into his mouth to stop himself.

'Oh, someone in the third year. His brother gets it.'

'Well, don't *ever* bring it into this house again!' and she tore it into several pieces and threw them in the kitchen pedal-bin.

'Mum, I was supposed to give that back.'

'Too bad. It should never have come home in the first place. Now then, what's this?'

'It's about the Dewsbury Bequest competition. We all got one, at the end of school.'

Moira read it through carefully while Tim and Frank sat and stared at each other in silent embarrassment. 'Well, this is a bit of a change, I must say. Your school's actually *thinking* for once. I hope you'll go in for this, Tim. It's not the money I care about, it's the principle of the thing. A really concentrated piece of work'd do wonders for you. Did you know that? Get you to sharpen up your approach a bit. Had any ideas yet?'

'Sort of,' he said unwillingly.

'Come on then, let's hear them.'

'Well, what about the Nine Standards? They're part of the town's history, aren't they? I could make it, well, like, historical . . .'

'Don't say "like", Tim, it's bad English. Yes, well, that's certainly one idea. Your father's got that book about them, you could start by reading it.'

'What are the Nine Standards?' Frank said.

Moira looked at him rather pityingly. 'Heavens, you a local boy and you ask me that?'

'They're the standing stones on Darnley Moor,' Tim interrupted hurriedly. 'My dad and I walked up to look at them the other week.'

'Oh, you mean where the witches hang out? I didn't know they were called that. We just say the Stones round here.'

'*Witches*?' Mrs Manning-Sanders seemed very interested all of a sudden. With those dark eyes and that fierce stare, she looked a bit witchy herself.

'Well, last year there was a bit of a fuss. Some funny women went up there and burned something. It was in all the papers.'

'What did they burn?'

Frank hesitated. 'Er, a sort of dummy, a man. It was part of what they believed like.'

'I see. Well, I'll obviously have to look into this a bit more.' She seemed to approve of the Darnley Witch Women and their anti-man campaign. With luck she might go and join them, then Tim'd have a break from all this nagging.

'I've got to go actually,' Frank said, putting his knife and fork together neatly and standing up.

'Oh dear, must you?' But he suspected that she couldn't wait to get him off the premises. She wanted to have a proper go at Tim about those tests. Then she'd get his project organized no doubt, then his music practice. The worst of it was that she didn't seem to *like* Tim at all. He wasn't a human being, just a disagreeable necessity to be slotted into a timetable. No wonder he was so nervous.

Their Dad never went on at them like that; he just loved them and thought they were wonderful. Dad had a big heart. Perhaps things might be better in this house if Tim's father was around a bit more. He went away a lot and left Mrs Manning-Sanders to organize everything, according to Tim. Perhaps that's why she was so bossy.

'Where do you live, Frank? she asked him, as she followed him into the hall.

'Bailey Street.'

'Oh, very nice. I wanted a town house when we bought this place. I believe people should live in cities, not on the fringes like this. But I lost the battle as usual.'

'But this house is lovely,' Frank said. He was puzzled. How could she say Bailey Street was 'very nice'? Two-up, two-down with Rochdale Road at the back, no garden and a chippy three doors down. Then he realized, she must think they lived in Baillie Terrace. Now that was beautiful, an elegant Georgian row in a square just behind the parish church. Those houses were the most expensive in Darnley.

'Mr Tanner's in the electrical business,' Tim said.

'And doing well obviously, with that address. How many outlets has he got?'

'Oh, just the one.' In their front room. But he wasn't telling her that, or about where they actually lived.

'He's getting one of Dad's loans, to expand,' Tim explained.

'And how much –'

'Sorry, but I really am late. See you then, Tim,' and Frank picked up his bag. He was going, before it all became too difficult.

'Do come again, won't you, Frank?' This was Moira, already clearing the decks, prior to grilling poor Tim on a spit.

'Well, yes, and thanks very much for the tea.'

61

Half-way across the estate he went over a bump and his bike chain broke. He decided to push it home. It was a messy job, fixing it together again; Dad usually did it for him. He didn't want to hang about on Larkfield now, anyway, it was getting dark.

As he was going past the row of shops on Sedgefield Avenue, he saw the man with the birthmark again. Same gear – dark anorak, dark jeans, suede shoes. A red scarf draped round his neck was the only new addition; perhaps he'd had a birthday. He'd just come out of Merrick's second-hand shop, the one that sold irons and hoovers to people who couldn't afford new. Dad didn't deal with that shop. He said most of the stuff in it had fallen off the back of a lorry.

Frank was on the other side of the road when he saw him. He stayed where he was, pretending to fiddle with the broken chain, but keeping one eye on what the man was doing. He wasn't carrying anything but he'd got money in his hand. After counting it (six notes at least, brown, so they must be tenners), he tucked them into a side pocket, zipped it up and walked off past the shops, along for a little way, then turning left into Lime Walk.

Frank leaned his bike against a fence. Nobody was going to get very far on it, with the chain broken. He walked rapidly down towards the junction, then he peered into the murk. Foxy was half-way along the street already, walking fast, he could just make out the red scarf bobbing up and down. Then he went into one of the houses.

Frank waited, one eye on his bike, but the man didn't come out again. He must remember Lime Walk though, for future reference. Just where he'd turned in, there was a white Mini with two wheels missing. That was a good marker, Lime Walk, Larkfield, Sign of the Clapped-out Mini.

He walked a few yards towards it, just to get the feel of the place before going back to his bike. This had got to be one of the worst roads on the whole estate. 'Lime

Walk' spoke of summer, of birds singing, of cool delicious drinks. But the actual place was a disaster area. These houses were the oldest on Larkfield and three-quarters of them were boarded-up and abandoned. Here and there he saw lights, and the faint blue flickering of a television, but the general feel was awful. Jungle gardens full of rubbish and smelly dustbins, collapsed cars like the white Mini slewed across the pavements, dog dirt every other step. Bailey Street, where the Tanners lived, might not be Baillie Terrace but it was miles better than this. As he turned away he heard a baby crying in one of the houses. The desolate little sound really upset him.

As he trudged home he thought again about Foxy, those neat sharp features, that hair, the birthmark on the neck, and the face nagged him. Where, oh where, had he seen it before? It was only when he was walking down Bailey Street that it came to him at last, a really awful thought that he was going to put firmly out of sight and out of reach, and never examine again. Wasn't that identikit picture in all the post offices just a bit like the man outside Merrick's? The pinched nose and mouth, the sticky-out cheek bones?

Come off it, Frank. There was no way this man who probably just did a bit of light thieving to make ends meet was the Larkfield Killer. He wasn't starting on that again. Dad had told him how he used to 'romance' when he was little, make up amazing stories about himself that didn't have a grain of truth in them. Now the 'romancing' had turned into the odd fib, and the occasional 'borrowing' of something he wanted very much. His heart thumped when he thought of how he'd 'borrowed' one of Tim's holiday photos. What would Sister Maggie think of a boy who did things like that? And the lovely Cass?

In the back room at home the lovely Lesley was sitting on Slob's knee. Telly was on full blast but nobody was watching it. The lovebirds were arguing about the parking ticket because Malc wanted to get away without paying and Lesley said he couldn't. Dad was staring at the screen where the Flintstones were having their own arguments with granite clubs. There was a letter in his hand with a familiar yellow eagle stamped on the top, the logo of the Friendly Northern Bank. So he'd heard, then.

'No go, son,' but he didn't have to say it. His face told everything; Frank had never seen him so depressed.

'Well, never mind, Dad,' he whispered, sitting down on the arm of his chair. 'Perhaps you can get a loan from somewhere else. Lots of places do them nowadays.'

'My father knows a man who lends money out, Mr Tanner.' This was Lesley from the settee. Frank didn't actually have anything against her. She'd always been quite nice to him. It was just that he felt fat girls might suffocate him. He didn't much care for the purple and yellow hairdo either; he liked quieter colours himself.

'Oh, no thanks, Lesley,' Dad said. 'It's all right, don't go worrying your father. I'm writing back to the Northern anyhow. It's discrimination, that's what it is.'

'Discrimination? What do you mean, Dad?'

Mr Tanner looked slightly embarrassed.

'C'mon,' Slob said. 'That's daft, Pa. What have they got against you?'

'I'm Irish. Well, my name's Irish. That's what I think, that they won't give me the loan because Feargus sounds too Irish.'

'Oh, *Dad*.'

'That's bloody ridiculous.'

'It's not, Malcolm, you'd be surprised. And don't swear. No, if I don't get satisfaction soon I'll – I'll mount a campaign against them. Not just the Friendly Northern either, the big ones. They're all in it together, you know. They're not interested in the little investor. Those TV ads are all talk.'

Frank had a sudden vision of his father taking on the whole might of Barclays Bank, and the Midland, and

Lloyds with its black horse. The picture wasn't very convincing. If Dad had not looked so upset, he'd have tried to make a joke about it.

'Well, I think you're bleedin' crazy,' Malcolm grunted.
'I said don't *swear*.'

'Er, Frank,' interrupted Lesley, sensing a storm brewing. 'I think one of your cats is expecting. Have you noticed?' She got off Slob's knee, picked up Flump 1 and brought her over to him. 'See, have a feel. I'd say she was having two or three. Our Mutt always gets like that.'

Gingerly, Frank let his fingers trample in the grey furry stomach. It definitely felt a bit lumpy. But the cat didn't like the impromptu medical examination. It yowled, jumped on to the floor, and shot under the dresser. Lesley was probably right then. Oh, heck.

'They were having their operations next week,' he told her. It was all arranged. Number 1 couldn't go now though, surely, it'd be murder. 'Are you certain?' he said.

'Well, our Mutt –'
'I think it's disgusting.'
'Don't be silly, Malcolm, it's only nature.'
'Look, Les, they're brother and sister. You think about it.'

Trust him to concentrate on the sex angle. Frank lifted Flump 2 on to his knee and stroked him. The proud father looked fit and well and very pleased with himself. It was all right for him; it was Number 1 that needed care and attention now. Would she be sick every morning like Karen Allcock's mum, at their school? Would she have those special food cravings? It might be quite interesting, looking after her till the kittens were born. A tiny bit of Frank felt quite pleased.

After the lovebirds had rattled off to Lesley's in the rusty Renault 4, he showed Dad the official form about the Dewsbury Bequest. 'I could win a hundred quid,' he said. Then he added, 'That'd help with the business, wouldn't it?' The money was really for his new room but Dad needed cheering up.

'Not really, son. It's thousands I need. Still, you have a go. Got any ideas?'

Frank told him about his newspaper project. 'The aim would be to look at all the local papers, you know, going back quite a few months, and to write up what they tell you about Darnley, people winning medals and saving people from fires and living to a hundred, that sort of thing. There are all those old newspapers down the cellar. They'd be worth looking at for a start. What d'you think, Dad?'

Mr Tanner leaned forward and squeezed his arm. 'I think it's a great idea, son. I could help you in the evenings. We could –'

'No, Dad, no help allowed. It says that on the form.' But he was thinking gloomily that some people would get 'unofficial' help, like the electric typewriter Tim was going to type his out on, and Amy Chauncey hinting that she might be able to borrow a word processor, from her dad's works. What real chance did the Tanners have?

'Some people will get their parents to help, you know,' he said aloud. 'It's not fair.'

'Oh, nothing's fair, son. My loan's not fair. I'm writing to that Mr Brocklehurst at the bank again tomorrow.'

It was no good Frank saying 'don't'. His father was in a really peculiar mood about this money business, all turned in on himself and broody. He'd now waste a lot of time writing letters and get absolutely nowhere. But telling him not to was obviously useless. It was quite clear that he regarded this standard refusal from the Friendly Northern as a personal insult. The Irish thing was ridiculous but Dad was a bit like that. Just occasionally he got these peculiar bees in his bonnet, and once they were there you couldn't shift them. It was like Malc, going on about traffic wardens.

'Want me to post this for you?' On the mantelpiece there was an envelope in his father's handwriting, addressed to the *Spotlight*.

'Are you going out?'

'Could do. It'll get the last post if I take it now.' Frank was ninety-nine per cent certain it was an ad for the Lonelyhearts Club, but he couldn't say anything. His father didn't know he knew. He couldn't imagine how he'd feel if Dad found a sincere lady for a lasting relationship; pushed out, probably. But he was so gloomy these days. Anything to cheer him up.

'Dad?' he said, putting his anorak on, 'you know Merrick's on Sedgefield Avenue? Well, if some of the stuff they sell is nicked, how come the police never get on to it?'

'They do, sometimes. But I reckon whoever runs that kind of business keeps the stuff for a while, before trying to get rid of it, till all the fuss has died down. Now that's something you could write about, thieving in Darnley, crime in "Our Town". There's enough of it going on,' he added miserably.

'Bit depressing, though.'

He picked up Dad's letter and went out through the front door. His father had mentioned the very thing that was bugging him, that furtive-looking individual with the red hair and the birthmark. If only Lord Dewsbury was offering a hundred pounds for a crime story. 'The Man with the Birthmark' by Frank Tanner. It sounded really good, that did.

Still, his father thought his newspaper idea was great. It'd be marvellous if he won the hundred pounds. And why shouldn't he? Miss Halliwell had told them the most important thing was to work it out yourself, which was exactly what he planned to do.

As he dropped the *Spotlight* letter into the box on the corner, he felt quite hopeful again, and he wished the envelope all the best as it disappeared. He was quite desperate for his father to cheer up a bit. So much so that, if he'd been Sister Maggie, he might well have said a little prayer.

Chapter Six

On the Saturday he saw her again, not when he did his
round though, it was still dead quiet at half past seven
when he walked up the drive. Perhaps they were all
busy praying. Cassie's house was like the grave too, not
even the whisper of a violin being practised. He'd have
given a lot for a sight of Cass, in a beautiful housecoat
perhaps, with her hair all down her back. But it sounded
particularly silent inside 103. They'd probably gone
away for the weekend. Tim had told him they owned a
holiday cottage in the Lake District.

After dinner Dad had told him he was going shopping
for the afternoon. 'What for?' Frank had asked him. He
knew his father had taken fifty pounds out of the Leeds
that morning; he'd looked in the deposit book.

'Oh, this and that,' was the vague reply. But he'd got
a familiar stubborn expression on his face. Frank
obviously wasn't going to be told what the money was
for. It might be to buy new clothes of course, in the hope
that his Lonelyhearts ad would come up trumps. If it
was, Frank approved. Dad never bought himself anything new and all the clothes he had were wearing out.

'I thought I'd go up to Tim's for a bit. OK?'

'Sure. Doing anything in particular?'

'No, just messing about.'

'All right, son. You'll be back for tea, won't you? Your
Gran said she might bring a casserole round.'

Oh no. The steak and kidney pie he'd had to force down after Moira's tea-party had been up to its usual standard and it had lain on Frank's feeble stomach all night, like a twenty-pound weight.

'I don't much like Gran's stews, Dad,' he muttered.

'Oh, come on, son. It's very good of her. She's seventy-four, you know, and she's not very well.'

Frank and his father didn't see eye-to-eye about Gran Corcoran. He wanted to like her more than he did, but she'd always been a bit cold with him. Slob was her favourite, not Frank. Somehow, though it wasn't exactly his fault, he thought it must be because his mum had died having him. She'd been Gran's daughter, when all was said and done.

He reckoned she thought Malcolm had been affected more than him, that it was the reason for his moods and bad tempers, Mum dying and everything. 'What you've never had you never miss,' she'd once told Frank. He thought that was a really daft thing to say, and he didn't like her brand of 'religion' either. It was a bit spooky. It involved playing cards and tea-leaves with messages in them, and getting through to the 'Other Side' to talk to people that were dead. He was certain Sister Maggie wouldn't approve of that sort of thing at all.

When he knocked at the door of the SLG house, it was opened a crack by a little old nun who only came half-way up his chest. If it hadn't been for the familiar purple uniform, he'd have definitely said it was one of the gnomes. She beamed when she saw him, revealing a perfect set of gleaming false teeth, and opened the door properly. 'It's Frank, isn't it? Sister Mary Magdalen's in the garden, I'll just fetch her,' and she disappeared down the long cool hall, silently, as if she was on oiled runners.

How did she know his name? Frank felt rather suspicious. Did it mean they'd been saying some prayers, in spite of what Maggie had promised? Names were important in religion, so were candles, and there was evidence of

69

both in this place. As he waited in the hall his eyes took everything in, all the religious paintings with candles lit underneath them, paintings in corners and at the turn of the stairs, even a painting in a dark little niche by the coat-pegs where it was much too dark to see properly.

He bent down and squinted at it. The picture under the stairs was tiny, in a thick gold frame, and the face of the Virgin it portrayed was beautiful. Her hands were pressed together in prayer and she had a gently smiling look; she wasn't fat and self-satisfied like the one by the phone – in fact she looked a tiny bit like Cassie Manning-Sanders.

He was still looking at the picture when he heard Maggie giggling in the distance. First the gnome, Sister Ursula of the Teeth, reappeared, then Maggie pulling mucky old gloves off. She'd been out in the garden, she explained, putting a few plants in that someone had given them.

'I just brought the white spirit,' Frank said. At home he'd said he was going to Tim's when that hadn't been his intention at all. It wasn't very honest of him to mislead Dad but he'd have thought it peculiar, Frank visiting a load of nuns. And he wanted to; he was interested in this place and he really liked Maggie.

'Well, thanks, Frank, that's really kind.' She grinned at him and took the bottle. Sister Ursula smiled too, and her false teeth slipped slightly. The yellow paint stains had gone, he noticed, but Maggie still went off dutifully to the kitchen to clean her hands. 'Just sit in the day room for a minute,' she said. 'See if you can get a word out of Eric for me, he's not spoken all day. He's in one of his moods. He doesn't like "silly women", he's just told me,' and she laughed.

It was very quiet in the big yellow room. If the other old men had been up, on the cadge, they'd obviously shoved off again, back to the hostel in town. Only Eric was left, in a ring of empty chairs, staring at a blank television screen.

Frank edged up to him. He still smelt awful and the lip was pushed out to maximum, but there was something else. His faded little eyes were all glossy, like Maggie's new paint. He was crying as he sat there staring into nothing, the tears running silently down his cheeks.

'What's up, Eric? Can I get you anything?' Frank plucked nervously at his dirty old cardigan. This was awful.

The old man didn't reply, but he must have heard because he shook his head and whispered, 'It's all right, chuck. It just comes over me. I'll be all right.' The voice was unexpectedly gentle. *Chuck* . . . that was what old Lancashire people said. Frank liked it.

'Can I get you anything?' he repeated, pulling up a chair and sitting down beside him. 'Is there anything you need . . . a drink or something?' The tears were running faster now, down the crumpled old cheeks, and Eric was making little dry sobbing noises. Frank hated it when grown-ups cried. Dad had done it once, about his mother.

'Can't have no drink here, mate,' the old man sniffed. 'Shouts blue murder, that one does, if you come round with a bottle.'

'I meant a cup of tea,' Frank whispered. 'They've always got a kettle on the go in the kitchen. They're really nice here.'

Privately, he thought they were more than 'really nice', putting up with people like Eric, not just 'putting up' either, but being really kind to them when all they got in return was bad temper and foul looks. This was the 'love of God', like it said on the gate.

Secretly, Frank felt slightly muddled about God, but what the nuns did felt more real than what Gran believed. It was love in action.

'I need . . . I need . . . ' said Eric, suddenly clutching himself between the legs.

'Come on then, I'll take you,' and Frank helped him

out of his chair. At least he could save the nuns this bit. He just hoped they'd get there in time.

He'd seen a door marked WC at the end of the hall, near the Cassie-madonna painting. He stood outside while the old man shuffled in. 'Well, you can shut the door, mate,' he said grumpily. Frank had left it open an inch, just in case Eric collapsed. He was a bit bluish round the mouth, like Gran Corcoran. Heart trouble, that was.

While he was waiting, Maggie came out of the kitchen. 'He was crying,' he said in embarrassment. 'I didn't know what to do. Then he suddenly had to go to the – you know. So I thought I'd better go with him. He doesn't look very well to me.'

She smiled at him. 'That was really good of you, Frank. He won't let any of us help him and he has little accidents. I'm a real expert with the mop and bucket these days.'

'What's up with him then, why was he crying?'

'Oh, he just sits and thinks about the past, and it all gets a bit much. He did have a nice wife, you know, and a good job, once. It was all OK till she died. After that, I think he gradually lost his grip on everything. There's no family, you see. I'm sure he wasn't always like this.'

Frank helped Eric back to his seat in the day room, then went out and left Maggie with him. Something, probably all these virgins and childs, had made him think of poor old Eric as he must have been once, a baby in a cradle. His mother had looked after him then, presumably, and loved him, then his wife who'd died – now he needed loving and looking after again. It was a good thing people like Sister Maggie were around to feed him and clean him up. He did hope she wasn't getting sworn at, in there. He'd tell the old man off, if he heard any of that going on.

She was certainly taking her time. Frank mooched about, looking at the pictures. That little madonna painting really was in a daft place, half hidden by purple macs. It should go on its own, on a plain white wall, with a spotlight shining on it. He put out a hand and fingered the thick gilt frame. It was really very beautiful . . .

'Come on, now, Eric, nothing's that bad,' Maggie was saying from the day room. 'Let me make you a cup of tea; it's a whole lot better for you than whisky. I'll be back in a few minutes.'

She'd found a nice piece of pine boarding for Frank to paint 'Sisters of the Love of God' on, and she said the nuns would pay for the materials, if he told them how much. The plank was quite big so he fixed it on to the carrier behind his bike saddle.

She waved him off down Palace Road, calling after him that she hoped he'd come back and see them very soon, that there was no hurry for the notice. But he couldn't wave back. He'd got one hand managing his bike and the other keeping the madonna picture from slipping down through his anorak, where he'd hidden it.

There was nobody in at home, so he went straight down to the cellar. Only when he'd switched the light on and bolted the door behind him did he feel able to take Maggie's picture out, and even then he couldn't really look at it. His hands were shaking too much.

Why had he done such a ridiculous thing, nicking a religious painting from a nunnery? Frank knew he wasn't honest 'through and through', not like Dad wanted him to be, and yet he couldn't help himself. There were the white lies now and again, like when he did badly in class but said he'd done well, and the greyer untruths too, like not letting on to the Manning-Sanderses that they didn't actually live in Baillie Terrace, and making out that Dad was a prosperous businessman. He'd nicked that photo of Cass as well. Why did he do such stupid things, and what would Maggie say if she ever found out?

He ought to get back on his bike straight away, go

back to Palace Road and replace the picture when there was nobody around. But somehow he couldn't. What if one of the nuns was lurking by the coat-pegs and caught him redhanded?

On the damp flaking wall over the rusty gas-fire he noticed a big nail sticking out. He felt behind the picture, found a wire, reached up and slipped it into position. Then he carefully angled the feeble 40-watt bulb on to the praying Virgin.

It looked beautiful, even in this damp cellar, and the face had a marvellous peace about it. You couldn't imagine somebody with that face ever saying anything nasty, or even thinking it. The simple blue robe the madonna was wearing fell down from her neck in a hundred little folds, like water running over rocks. It was the loveliest thing Frank had ever seen in his life, that's why he'd wanted it. There was nothing beautiful at all in 14 Bailey Street. It was neat and tidy enough but not beautiful. And something deep inside him needed beauty, like a thirsty man needs water.

Dad had obviously been home and gone out again because the cellar floor was stacked high with tins of paint. Frank glanced at them without much interest. The paint would be for a home-decorating job he was doing for someone. It brought extra money in, though he often had to work evenings to get finished. There was an awful lot of paint though, and it was gloss, a bright green colour called Buckingham. Who'd want their entire house done in that?

Then Frank had a thought. He could use a drop of it for Maggie's notice. First he'd paint the piece of wood white, then he'd do 'Sisters of the Love of God' in bright green capitals. He could make the notice tonight, wrap it up really nicely and take it over to the SLG house as a surprise. That would make up a bit for nicking their picture. Not that he was keeping it for very long; he just needed to wait for the right moment to slip it back.

Another thought struck him as he stared at the picture. Why had he always assumed that this gas-fire was broken? He got matches from the kitchen and tried lighting it. It came to life straight away with little popping noises, then settled down to a nice gentle hiss.

Great. A fire would dry this place out in no time and it wasn't all that small. With his paper-round money he could buy plants to put in the old stone sink in the corner. He could buy trendy bedding too, like Tim's, and they could redecorate. There was paint and stuff down here already. Dad stored a lot of his things in the cellar. He could slap a bit on right now, just to see how it looked.

Half an hour later he was standing in front of the hissing gas-fire, wiping his hands on a rag. He'd painted the whole chimney-breast Brilliant White Matt, and it looked fabulous. The Virgin looked fabulous too.

Things were starting to hum now, and he was getting a little warm happy feeling inside. There was no reason at all why this quiet basement room shouldn't become his personal, private den. It wouldn't cost all that much and Slob would be delighted if Frank moved out of the front bedroom. More room for his own mess then, and to snog with Lesley in private. Meanwhile, Frank could sort himself out down here. He always felt better when he was properly organized. This new room would give him a new start to everything. When it was finished he'd invite Tim round. He might even have a little party.

Over his head the front door banged. 'Frank? Are you back? Where are you, son?'

'Down here, Dad, I'm just coming up.'

Frank whipped the Virgin off her hook, wrapped her in his anorak and stuffed her under the sink among the cobwebs. Then he ran upstairs two steps at a time; he didn't want any awkward questions.

But Mr Tanner had a keen nose. 'I can smell gas,' he said, 'and paint. What have you been up to?'

'I was just in the cellar. I got the gas-fire going and I slapped a bit of that white emulsion on.'

'What for?'

'Well . . . just to try.'

'Try what?'

'I wanted to clean the place up a bit. I thought if –'

'Now look, Frank, I've told you before, that cellar's too damp. You'd end up with rheumatic fever if you slept down there.'

'But someone must have, once. There's a fire and everything.'

'That was for when they did the washing.'

'It'd still be OK, Dad. I'm fed up of having to share with Malcolm.'

'Listen, son, stick with it for the time being. OK? We'll sort something out.'

'*What* though?'

'Well, something. Now listen, I'm going out again, after I've freshened up. Got any plans yourself?'

'Not really. I'll probably stay in and watch telly. Where are you off to then?'

'Oh, just out. I'll probably end up at the Munns'.'

Mr and Mrs Munn were a decrepit old couple who lived at the top of Bailey Street. Dad kept an eye on them and did odd jobs round the house. He obviously wasn't going there first though, he'd said 'end up'.

'Where else are you going?'

'Just out.' His father sounded quite prickly now and it wasn't like him. But it couldn't be a Lonelyhearts date yet, could it? The ad wouldn't be printed till next week.

'OK, OK,' He wasn't asking any more questions about Dad's comings and goings. If he and Slob were out all evening, at least he could make a start on Maggie's notice. There was his project too. All the old newspapers needed sorting out.

'Dad?' he said suddenly. 'What's all that paint doing in the cellar?'

'Er, it's for a decorating job.' But his father's voice was definitely peculiar now, and he'd gone a bit pink.

76

'Who on earth wants their house painting that colour? And it's gloss.'

'I know it's gloss, but the customer's always right, isn't he? Now I'm going up to have a quick wash. Why don't you put the kettle on?'

Soon Frank was on his own again with the whole evening stretched out before him, and Dad walking down Bailey Street on his secret mission. If it wasn't to do with his Lonelyhearts ad, then it was something to do with those cans of green paint. *What* though? Dad had his odd little ways but this time Frank was absolutely stumped.

It was the usual Saturday night rubbish on telly so he switched it off and started looking at the old newspapers he'd brought up from the cellar. Most of them were copies of the *Darnley Examiner*. Frank read through a couple then decided he'd better have a plan before going any further. He could cut out the interesting bits and divide them into sections. What did the local paper tell you about life in 'Our Town'? That was going to be the subject of his Dewsbury project, and he thought it was a pretty good one. At the same time, though, he was keeping his eyes open for anything to do with house breaking.

He worked steadily for a whole hour with Flump 1 curled up on his knee. From time to time he fed her cheese and onion crisps from a bag. By eight o'clock the kitchen table was covered with newspaper cuttings, but this was only the start. Now he'd got to think of some interesting headings. 'Verve, originality and spark' – that's what Miss Halliwell had said the judges would be looking for. With her crushed-in face and her lumpy old clothes, the poor woman had got about as much spark as a wet firework. This idea would take off on its own anyhow. He could manage without teachers, he'd decided.

He sat back and tickled Flump 1's ears. So what did

all these old *Examiners* tell you about life in Darnley-in-Makerfield? Well, for a start, people seemed to live very long lives in 'Our Town'. There was no end of golden weddings, and dozens of photos of couples with names like 'Wilfred and Lena' and 'Duggie and Alice', all grinning over floral tributes from their seventeen great-grandchildren.

'Spell that lingers on after 50 years' ran one headline. 'A call for help to remove a wooden spell (old Darnley word for 'splinter') from a friend's leg, cast a charm that was to last over 50 years.' 'Still in tandem after 50 years' another boasted. This pair had started their romance in a chip shop on Haymarket Street, then gone cycling together. After their marriage, it explained enthrallingly, 'the happy couple transferred to a tandem.'

The editor wasn't just obsessed with old age though; he'd clearly got an eye for the odd and peculiar too. 'Sticking plaster found in pork pie' was a good headline. Even better was the one that said 'Woman's head found in garden.' It was maddening but half the report was missing. Frank was never going to find out who owned that decomposed head.

He got a piece of paper, cut it up and began to make labels. 'Getting Old in Darnley' went on top of the golden weddings pile, and 'Getting Ill in Darnley' went on top of the pork-pie article. Under 'Getting Buried in Darnley' went the best cutting so far. It was headed 'Constable's Coffin Conundrum' and it read: 'A brand-new coffin, found abandoned on the moors above Darnley-in-Makerfield, is baffling police and undertakers in north-west Lancashire. The varnished box, lined with pink plush, was discovered by farmer Eddie Wardle who was checking sheep on the slopes below Blackstone Edge. Inside the coffin police found an Indian takeaway meal, yards of computer tape and three books of Co-op stamps.'

After the Golden Oldies section his biggest was definitely going to be Crime. 'Getting Ripped Off in Darnley'

Frank printed laboriously, though he'd already decided that he'd have to think of a more official way of putting it. Teachers always told you off for 'slang', even when it was the clearest way of saying something.

As he leafed through his cuttings he kept thinking of the man with the birthmark. Most of these 'crimes' were a bit pathetic really. Why risk going to prison for the sake of a second-hand toaster and a tin of ham? But that's what had disappeared in one 'robbery'. You could always get second-hand toasters on Darnley Market. *Where did they come from*? Did the Foxys of this world keep the stallholders in steady supply?

Before putting everything away in the new blue folder provided by Miss Halliwell, Frank took a sheet of paper and drew a little map. Something else had emerged from looking at these cuttings, a sort of pattern. In the last eighteen months there'd been a whole spate of petty break-ins in the northern part of the town, some in houses not far from Bailey Street, some on Larkfield and quite a few just across the dual carriageway, on the edge of Denning. What struck him was that they were nearly all *electrical* robberies, even in Denning where people must have canteens of silver cutlery, golf and tennis trophies and valuable jewellery. The things that had been pinched were nearly always mixers and food-processors, radios and hair-driers, things that weren't too bulky to handle and easily got rid of, especially to a dodgy-looking shop like Merrick's on Sedgefield Avenue.

If the man with the birthmark was out of work and strapped for cash, he could easily keep himself going by helping himself to the odd electrical goody in a house where the owners had thoughtfully forgotten to lock up. And he'd definitely looked suspicious that day Frank had nearly run over him, suspicious *and* guilty. There was the bit of wire too, and that first sighting when he'd been sussing out the houses on Palace Road.

Then he thought further. Crimes like these were ten

a penny in the *Examiner*, and they weren't just confined to the area north of Bailey Street either. As Frank clipped his map to the robbery cuttings, a really terrible thought suddenly occurred to him. *What if Dad, in desperation about money, had started nicking electrical things himself?* It would certainly explain his funny, shifty mood this evening. It might have been nothing to do with that paint in the cellar. He might be sussing out likely houses at this very minute.

He stood up, sweeping all the papers together and letting Flump 1 drop to the floor with an aggrieved squalk. *No*, never, never, never could such a thing be true of his father. Reading all these crummy news stories in one go was making him lose his grip on reality.

It was 'reality' though; Jack and Annie still cycling together after fifty glorious years, and leaving your Indian takeaway in a coffin on Blackstone Edge. Frank cleared the table and tried to think positively. He'd had a profitable hour's work on his school project and Dad's private affairs had nothing whatever to do with him. But he was definitely going to keep his eye on Foxy, he decided. He made a big label, printed 'THE MAN WITH THE BIRTHMARK' on it, stuck it on an envelope and put all the robbery cuttings inside.

As he was feeding Flump 1 the remains of the crisps, the phone rang in the hall and he ran to answer it. It just might be Wedding Dress Wendy to say he could do a Sunday round tomorrow. She'd promised she'd do what she could.

'Hello. Is that Frank?' The voice on the other end was cheerful and bouncy.

'Yes. Who's that?'

'It's Number Ten Downing Street.'

'You what?'

'It's Maggie, Frank, Maggie from Palace Road.'

Oh, heck. His hand started to shake and he had to grip the receiver tighter, in case he dropped it. She was going to ask him about the picture. *She knew.*

'Listen, will you be doing your round tomorrow?'

'Er, no, I don't think so.' Another white lie. He'd told her he definitely *was* getting a Sunday round, because just two delivery days a week sounded a bit pathetic and he wanted to impress her. He really would have to stop misleading people.

'Oh, well, never mind. I was going to say drop in, if you're passing. I wanted to ask you something.'

So she did know. 'What?' Frank said. He'd got to get it over with.

'Nothing important. Listen, call in if you're passing. They're back next door by the way. I've seen your friend Tim.'

'OK. I might.'

'Bye then, Frank, and God bless.'

'Maggie. Is Eric all right?' He'd not liked that blue round the mouth.

'Seems to be. He's taken quite a fancy to you. See you soon.'

Frank put the phone down in a state of confusion. Maggie seemed to know an awful lot about him, without actually having asked many questions. She knew he'd nicked the picture for one thing – and why had she mentioned his 'friend' Tim? It was really because she knew he admired Cass. 'Cass is back' was what she'd been trying to say. As for God 'blessing' him, well, you'd expect that from a nun. He'd rather she didn't say it, though, somehow it constituted interference. And she already knew what he thought about praying, he'd told her about his Gran.

As he stood there in the hall a newspaper plopped through the letter-box. It was the weekend *Examiner* from Midwood's newsagent's. Frank picked it up. They were very late tonight; Fat Lil would have something to say to her boys if they got behind like this. Perhaps, if she didn't give him another round, he'd see if Midwood's would take him on. They were obviously a bit sloppy, and a lot nearer home than Wendy News.

81

On the back of the *Examiner* he noticed a big feature about home improvements. 'Does your house look run down?' it said. 'If so, the Wall Doctor can put it right.' This firm could do anything, or so it claimed, sandblasting, brick replacement, damp-proofing. 'Ring 21284' it concluded 'and get a free estimate.' Underneath there was an ad for a monster bed sale at Austins in King Street. Their beds were so posh they were called 'sleep systems'. For a hundred pounds, 'while stocks last', he could get himself the very latest model, and pay off the rest in easy instalments. That figure rang a bell. All he had to do was to win the 'Our Town' competition.

What was the point of putting a de luxe bed down a mouldy cellar though? *Damp-proofing* . . . if he was serious about sleeping in the basement, and he was, they ought to start with basics. What was wrong with getting this Wall Doctor to give a free estimate? Dad wouldn't mind. Nervous, but with his head rapidly filling up with striped sheets and rubber plants and leather armchairs, Frank dialled the number and arranged for a Mr Stanley Arrowsmith to come and inspect the cellar at eleven next day. Dad always had a morning coffee with Gran on Sundays, and Slob was spending the weekend with Lesley.

The man had sounded very enthusiastic at first, but audibly less keen when he realized the Tanners lived in Bailey Street and not Baillie Terrace, where houses cost a bomb. There were quite a few snobs in Darnley, Frank had decided, going back to the sitting-room. That might be something else he could work into his 'Our Town' project.

Chapter Seven

Stanley Arrowsmith was definitely one of the snobs. He arrived at eleven o'clock sharp the next morning in a white mini-van with 'Wall Doctors Limited' painted on the side in blue, and stood on the front-door step jigging impatiently from one foot to the other. When Frank opened the door he stared right through him. His lips curved round and his mouth took on a nasty sneery expression.

What did he see? One lanky school kid, only twelve and three-quarters but looking quite a bit older, neatly dressed, clean-looking and politely spoken. But beyond him there was a shabby little hall and beyond that a cramped sitting-room where all the chairs were worn and shiny, the curtains cheap and thin and the telly in urgent need of updating. No hi-fi or video here, no snazzy little hatchback parked outside. The whole place was in need of a facelift and there was clearly no money to pay for it. The Wall Doctor walked straight in without being asked and asked rather snappily for 'the man of the house'. When told he'd had to go out and that Frank was 'deputizing', he got snappier still.

He condescended to have a look at the cellar but the whole visit took less than ten minutes. While he poked and prodded at the walls, took readings on a damp meter and let out a series of gloomy muttering noises, Frank stood watching, sinking steadily under a weight of black depression. His common sense told him that it would cost big money to make this place properly habitable. You could do anything if you had the cash, but the Tanners were broke.

And yet. Firmly fixed in his mind he'd got this tantalizing memory of Tim's wonderful basement den up in Palace Road. It was seeing that room which had started all this, started him plotting and planning, started him hoping. When something like that happened you couldn't go back, you had to do something about it.

He said timidly, 'How much do you reckon it would cost, then?'

'Depends on how far you want to go.'

'Well, to make this room habitable like?'

The man snapped his damp meter into its case, picked a hair off his suit and said, 'Five grand.'

'Five – *five thousand pounds*? Just to damp-proof one room?'

'Oh, come off it, damp-proofing's only the start. You've got big problems here. See those cracks? That's serious subsidence in my opinion. The whole front wall needs underpinning. We're talking about a lot of money, I'm afraid. Now then, do you want me to send your father an estimate? F. Tanner wasn't it?'

'Yes.' F for Frank and F for Feargus. 'But listen,' he said hastily, 'he'll ring if he wants one. It's rather more than we'd expected, you see.'

'All right. Suit yourself,' and the man made for the stairs without a backward glance.

When the white mini-van had driven off, Frank went back down the cellar. Late last night he'd come down here and painted Maggie's notice in secret. Although it was still a bit tacky, he was taking it round there today, to make up. He was returning the picture too, because the longer he hung on to it the worse the situation was going to get. Just how he was going to explain himself he'd not quite decided. He'd have to think about that on the way over.

The chimney-breast he'd painted the day before was dry now but stained faintly with brown. The wet had obviously started to come through already; that's how damp it was down here. As he felt under the sink for Maggie's picture something moved across his hand. *Ugh*. Frank withdrew it, his flesh creeping slightly, then stayed resting back on his haunches, absolutely still. After a minute something emerged from the shadows and hopped across the flagged floor towards the gas-fire. It was a massive green frog.

Within seconds he was back in the sitting-room, cuddling Flump 1. He needed something warm and furry in his lap, after a shock like that. If the cellar was so damp that frogs were breeding in it, then his scheme for a bedroom was hopeless. He might be snoozing down there one day, on his ultimate sleep system, and find them hopping about all over him. Then again, if Mr Wall Doctor was correct, a wall could collapse on him and he'd be buried alive.

Frank was getting gloomier by the minute now. Tim Manning-Sanders didn't know how lucky he was, never having to think about money. Life wasn't fair, him stuck here in Bailey Street with frogs in the cellar and Tim and Cass in Palace Road, with more money and space than they knew what to do with. *Not fair, not fair* . . . the words were dinning themselves into his brain now, like a set of jungle drums.

'Life's never fair, son.' (Dad, when the bank said No.)

'We've all got our cross to bear, Feargus.' (Gran, talking about his mother dying, when they thought he and Malcolm were out of earshot.)

When he'd told Maggie that he didn't think things were 'fair', she'd shrugged and said a very funny thing. 'God never promised us a rose garden, Frank.'

He still didn't know what it meant.

He wrapped her picture up in a plastic carrier and clipped it on to the back of his bike. The SLG notice he laid across the handlebars and kept in position with one hand, because it wasn't quite dry. Then he wobbled off in the direction of Denning.

On the way over he decided to check up on the man with the birthmark. Larkfield was even quieter than normal. Merrick's electrical shop was shut, barred and bolted, and the sweet shop next door had a heavy iron grille screwed to its windows. Round here people obviously expected break-ins; they must be part of the normal way of life.

The house marked by the Mini, where Foxy had turned in, was number 49, the left-hand one of a pair. It was set well back from the road at the end of a long narrow garden. Next-door's grass came up to Frank's knees and all its windows were boarded up, but 49 looked as if somebody still cared about it. The long strip of lawn was neatly trimmed and there were plants in the borders. Every curtain was still drawn across though, in spite of the fact that it was nearly midday. There were no gaps, so Frank couldn't do any spying.

Instead he crept up to the front door and listened. Someone was awake because he could hear a television. At the side of the house there was a motor bike, quite old but very well looked after, no rust on it hardly, and all the chromework nicely polished. This could well be Foxy's. He was a neat-looking individual, Frank remembered, and neatness in dress often extended to people's possessions. He was like that himself. In the back garden he could see a vegetable plot and long rows of bamboo canes. Neat and tidy again.

Then he heard voices inside the house, and a door opening, so he shot down the path and got back on his bike. He wasn't so sure now. Would somebody with the sleazy, thieving lifestyle he'd dreamed up for Foxy really live in a trim little house like this? It looked too organized, too respectable. Either he'd got the wrong place or the man with the birthmark had simply been visiting somebody at number 49. The third possibility was that

86

he was wrong on all counts. All he'd actually got against the man so far was that peculiar moment when he'd jumped away from the car, the piece of wire coat-hanger, and that time he'd come out of Merrick's with a load of ten-pound notes. Dad would say he was 'romancing' again.

The motor bike was worth remembering though; YLG 242X, blue with a white carrier on the back. If Malc had seen it he'd have reeled off the make, year and engine capacity straight away, whereas Frank was a dud when it came to things on wheels. He'd noticed one thing though. The white carrier had been plastered with coloured stickers: Superman, Spot the Dog and My Little Pony. A note about that would certainly go into his 'Man with the Birthmark' envelope, even if it didn't lead to anything.

When he got to Palace Road, the front door of 105 was wide open and two nuns were standing in the front garden, over a smoky bonfire. One was Maggie and the other was obviously Sister Geraldine, the person in charge, the fat one who'd shouted blue murder at Eric. She was tall with great beefy shoulders and her long habit looked like a vast purple tent. She was holding a clipboard and giving some instructions to Maggie, who stood poking at the bonfire with a stick, black wellies peeping out from underneath her purple hem. Frank left his bike by the gate with the picture still fixed on the back, and walked up the drive with his green and white notice. This definitely wasn't the moment to confess.

Sister Geraldine had a round red face, swollen, as if it had been boiled, and thick fleshy lips. Her eyes were a keen bright blue, the sort that didn't miss a trick. On her purple bosom there was a large silver crucifix, so large that he could see the hanging figure of Christ quite clearly, the tiny silver nails in the silver hands, the tiny silver drops of blood. She saw him staring at it and the big blubber lips smiled remotely.

'Er, I did you this,' he said, shoving the notice up at her. 'But it's still a bit tacky.'

Sister Geraldine inspected it carefully. 'How very, *very* kind, Frank,' she said warmly, 'and I do like the colour. Thank you so much.'

'That's OK. My dad had a bit of green paint.'

The fat nun *knew his name*, and that he'd *offered to do a sign*. They were obviously all in league together at this place, discussing lost causes like paper boys and old men, and praying for them, no doubt.

The phone rang inside the hall and Sister Geraldine went to answer it. 'How are you, then?' Maggie said, concentrating on the burning leaves and not on him, as if she wanted to avoid their eyes meeting.

'I'm OK. Is that the boss then?'

'Yes, that's Sister Geraldine. She's lovely. Now listen, are you doing anything special?'

'What, now? No, not really.'

'Well, will you come for a walk with me? I've got some free time now, and it's a gorgeous day.'

'Er, OK then.' Frank felt trapped. She was obviously going to bring up the subject of the picture, while all the time it was on his bike, wrapped in its Tesco's plastic bag. But it was ages since he'd been up Darnley Moor and there it was, all goldy-green and stretched out invitingly behind the houses. You paid more to live in Palace Road because of the 'incomparable view'.

'Should I put my bike inside the gate?' he said.

'All right, and I'll go and change my shoes.'

While she was inside he shoved it out of sight under the big holly bush and put a hand out to release the plastic package from the carrier. Then he stopped. He just didn't have the guts to own up, and the nicer Maggie and Co. were to him, the harder the whole thing became. He dithered for ages by the sooty bushes, feeling all sweaty and hot.

Through the day-room window he could see Eric staring out. Old people spent a lot of time staring. Gran

88

Corcoran did it too. He waved, went up the drive and shouted 'Hello'. Eric pushed the window open. He looked quite pleased to see Frank.

'I like your sweater, Eric.' It was blue with jazzy green stripes and it was about ten sizes too big. 'Where've you nicked that from then?' (*Nicked*. He should talk . . .)

'Her in charge gave it me.'

'Well, I hope you said thank you.'

Eric just grunted and sucked air in through his false teeth. He was looking better though, pinker in the cheeks. Frank was relieved. He'd thought about him quite a bit since that scene in the day room, when he'd cried. The sheer helplessness of the lonely old man's plight had upset him somehow. It was the helpless tears, from someone who'd lived so long and ought to be in a nice flat somewhere, surrounded by his grandchildren. Then he heard Maggie call cheerfully, 'Are you ready then?' She was crunching across the gravel towards him, stout walking boots showing under the purple skirt.

'Behave yourself then, Eric!' and Frank grinned at the purple vision before him.

'And what are you laughing at?' she said.

'You look like Mickey Mouse in those.'

'How's your dad then?' Maggie asked, as they set off towards the moors. She said she hadn't realized you could get up there so quickly from Palace Road but Frank had shown her the short-cut, along the old farm track. Dad used to come along here with him and Malc but that felt like centuries ago. They didn't do family things any more. These days Slob always wanted his Sundays free for Lesley, and Dad didn't seem to have the heart for little expeditions. Bailey Street and its problems had become the limit of his universe.

'He's been acting a bit funny lately,' Frank said. It was a relief to tell somebody.

'Is the romance not going well then?'

'Oh, I don't think it's that. They've not even put his

89

ad in yet. No, I think it's this loan he wants from the bank. They've refused his application and he's taken it very personally. He thinks they won't give it him because he sounds Irish. His name's Feargus, you see. He's daft in some ways, my dad.'

Maggie burst out laughing. 'I love it,' she said. 'I'd quite like to meet him. He sounds fun.'

The deep rutted lane that led on to the open moorland had high tangled hedges still in their winter brown, but with faint green streaks where spring was pushing through. A bird was twittering somewhere and its thin, insistent cheep mingled with Maggie's peals of laughter. As they slogged uphill there was a sudden burst of sun. Frank's heart rose. It was good out here, he could breathe, even if he had stolen the picture and this nun was laughing at his dad's antics.

'How would you feel if he did get a girlfriend, Frank?' She'd obviously been thinking about it, perhaps in her praying sessions.

'Dunno, really.'

'Would you be jealous?'

'I don't think so. But it won't come to anything anyhow. He's had girlfriends before. He never gets anywhere with them.'

'I just wondered if . . . about your mother and everything, how you would, well, react.'

'What you've never had you never miss,' Frank said, a bitterness creeping into his voice. 'That's what my Gran once said. She prefers Slob to me.'

'That's ridiculous,' Maggie said passionately.

Yes, it was. He couldn't miss his mother the way Slob and Dad did; she was only a name on a gravestone to him. But he'd always missed *a* mother. Everyone needed a person to tell their troubles to, someone to ask how they'd got on, at the end of an ordinary day. That's why he enjoyed being with Maggie, he'd decided. She seemed to know the right questions to ask, and she actually listened to the answers. She was all soft in the middle too, like a chocolate.

'Mind if I say something, Frank, about your brother?'

He didn't reply, just shook his head as they negotiated the deep muddy ruts underfoot.

'Well, I'd not call him "Slob", if I were you.'

'Why not? He is one. You should see him when –'

'I know, Frank,' she interrupted, 'but if you could just bring yourself to view him as, well, a human being. I know he causes you problems but he's got them too, hasn't he? He must have, these nasty tempers you told me about. It's all to do with your mother dying so suddenly you know.'

'I don't see that it matters what I call him,' Frank said rather stormily. He wasn't sure he liked the way this conversation was going.

'I think it does. If you can't see any good in him then just pretend there is some. Do you understand what I'm getting at? It's like me and Eric. He's pretty awful to us at 105, I can tell you, worse than any of the others, but we've all talked about it and if we treat him as the nasty old thing he is, well, he'll just get nastier, won't he? It's surprising what a little love can do. It can change people in the end.'

Ah yes, but she was a Sister of the Love of God, he was thinking defensively. Love . . . how could he ever 'love' Slob?

'All I'm saying is that if you think of Malcolm as a slob, then he'll behave like one. Try using his proper name.'

'Well, he calls me Our Kid.'

'You know I'm right. That's not half as bad as "Slob", is it, Frank? In fact, I quite like it. Come off it.'

They walked on in silence for a long time while Frank thought about Slob and Eric and the love of God. The farm lane had become a narrow, stony track now, swooping up and over the first big fold of Darnley Moor. When they'd gained a little more height they would come to the Stones. Maggie had never seen them before and she sounded excited at the prospect. He, Frank, would show her.

'Do you think your father would like to do some odd jobs for us, Frank, up at the house? He sounds quite a handyman. It all needs rewiring.'

'I could ask him.' But he didn't intend to. Number 105 Palace Road, Sister Geraldine, Ursula of the Teeth, and soft-centred Maggie were his, and special. He didn't want to share them with anybody else, not even Dad.

'Actually, it was Eric I really wanted to talk to you about,' she said next. Sweet relief flooded through him. So she hadn't got him up here to ask about the missing picture then.

'What about him?'

'Well, he's taken rather a fancy to you, and as I said, we do find him a bit difficult at times. Could you help?'

'What with?'

'If you could just come up, now and again, and sit with him, perhaps read him the paper. Take him to the loo, if you really don't mind. I'm a bit fed up of washing the floor.'

'Oh, I can do that.' He didn't much like the old man, in fact, he was a bit repulsive, but he did like Maggie, and it would be an excuse to go up there.

'We thought we might take him out one day, when the weather warms up, with some of his pals from the hostel. You could come.'

'Where were you thinking of going?'

'Well, he keeps talking about Blackpool. That's where he spent his honeymoon. It's a little dream he's got and he'll be eighty at Easter. It could be a birthday treat for him. Will you think about it?'

'OK, but I'm not really mad on Blackpool.' Gran Corcoran used to take him and Slob, sorry, *Malcolm*, there on day trips. It was all chip shops and arcades and the Golden Mile covered with wall-to-wall deckchairs. His memories were of constant drizzle, Malc in short pants running into all the lavatories along the promen-

92

ade and Gran getting anxious; pink rock that was supposed to say 'Blackpool' all the way through.

'I've never been to Blackpool myself,' Maggie said cheerily, 'but they say it's an experience.'

'It's that all right,' Frank said with some feeling. 'OK, I'll come if you really want me to.'

Funny how the Stones looked so small, now he was pushing five-foot nine, and not just small but tatty; a rough circle of knobbled granite humps, nine of them altogether, hunched round on the top of Darnley Moor like little old women having a good gossip. They'd been vandalized too, not just by people's initials but by white paint and rude messages. Did nuns know about four-letter words? Frank felt embarrassed and turned away.

As they stood there in the sunshine a group of walkers came puffing up from the other side of the grassy circle, where the moor dropped down sharply again, and separated themselves out to look at the Stones. A camera was produced from a leather case, a lens adjusted, a notebook opened. Then a familiar voice said, 'Right, now before we start, let's have a plan of action, shall we? If you're going to do this, Tim, I want you to do it properly.'

Frank retreated hastily, right back to the farm-gate they'd climbed over to get on to the open moor. He couldn't face the Manning-Sanderses at that moment, not while he was out on a walk with Maggie. They'd think it was peculiar. The whole family was there, Moira organizing Tim with his notebook and pencil, Jack obediently taking photos, and Cassie sitting on the sheep-bitten turf, lifting her face to the sun. She had someone with her too, a boy with curly fair hair and black glasses. Even from this distance Frank could see that they held hands, when Moira wasn't looking.

He watched Maggie go over to them and start talking, her head to one side slightly, in that bird-like way she had, then laughter rippling across to him, light laughter over the short springy grass. He turned his back on them all and waited. They had to be getting home anyhow, she'd told him she was due back by three o'clock.

'You're a funniosity, Frank Tanner,' she remarked, hitching her purple skirt up and scrambling over the gate. 'Why didn't you come and say hello? You know them.'

'Didn't feel like it, did I?' he muttered, setting off at top speed down the track. It wasn't just that they'd come on a walk together, him and a nun, it was Cass and that boy with the glasses. Even though she was older than he was, and there'd never been any real chance for him ever, he still couldn't bear it, now the cold hard facts were staring him in the face.

'Frank,' Maggie puffed, running to keep up with him, 'you look upset. What's wrong?'

'Oh, nothing. Well, I don't want to talk about it. I suppose they were telling you about the Dewsbury competition? Tim's doing his project on the Stones. They shouldn't be helping him, you know, it's not fair. And don't talk to me about rose gardens,' he added quite savagely.

'I wasn't going to,' she replied meekly. 'What's your topic anyway?'

'Local newspapers. Dad said I could do crime in Darnley but I thought that was too depressing. So I'm doing a bit of everything, to show what goes on round here like, in people's lives. You get some funny stories in local papers. At least I thought of it myself,' he said, suddenly belligerent. 'I won't win though.'

'Why not? Your topic sounds brilliant to me, and it's about what's happening *now*, not things that are millions of years old, like those Stones.'

'I never win anything.'

'Oh, rubbish, we've all got different talents, Frank, different gifts.'

'All right. What are mine then?'

She was thoughtful for a minute, then she said slowly, 'Well, I think you've got a gift for . . . for friendship.

94

Take Eric, for example – we can't get a civilized word out of him, but he's quite different with you.'

But it was Cassie Frank had been interested in, not smelly old Eric. She'd been a lovely thing in his drab life, a sunshiny place in his mind. Maggie was like a friendly big sister but with Cass, in spite of the age gap, he'd dreamed that something, some day, might have 'happened'. She was obviously spoken for though; she'd got a boyfriend. Everybody had got somebody. Dad was advertising for a woman, Malc had got Lesley, and Maggie had got God. Frank felt out in the cold.

'Talking of local crime,' she said slowly, as the lane flattened out and the backs of the Palace Road gardens came into view, 'somebody's been into our house, I'm afraid, and stolen something.'

'Oh . . . what?' Frank asked, and a cold creepy feeling came over him.

'Just a picture, a small madonna. It was at the back of the hall. The thing is, it's quite valuable. There's not very much of great value at 105 but that painting was worth quite a bit. It's very old.'

'Have you told the police?'

'Oh yes, but they didn't seem very interested. They have to deal with things like that day in day out, of course. Well, you'll know that, from your project.'

'Yes,' agreed Frank, but he had some trouble getting his words out. Sheer nerves had made his throat go all tight. He felt as if he'd swallowed a large pebble.

'Will you keep your eyes open for us?' she said, as they approached 105. 'You're up early, on your paper-round mornings. Let us know if you see anything unusual, won't you? Anyone hanging round for example.'

As they walked past the holly bush he could see the package still sitting there, behind the saddle. If only she'd not mentioned it, he might have had the courage to give it back, with some cock-eyed explanation which he hoped she'd accept. But he couldn't say anything now. It would have to go back home for a bit, and join the frogs in the cellar.

To make up he stayed for an hour and read the whole of the sports section to Eric, out of the weekend *Examiner*. It took ages too because the old man was deaf and Frank had to repeat half of it. This time they sat in the kitchen because Eric was having his feet washed by Maggie. The smell was awful, like old fish, and he wasn't a bit grateful. In fact, he kept complaining and poking at her as she bent over the plastic bowl, telling her to 'leave off'. 'Why can't the boy do it?' he said. Then he added 'Bloody women', under his breath.

'Because it's not his job. Now just pipe down or I'll send him home and we've not had the football results yet,' said Maggie smartly.

At least, when Frank had finished the paper and said he was off home, Eric had said 'Thanks, chuck' quite nicely. But Maggie didn't get any thanks at all, and it was pretty basic, washing a smelly old man's rotting feet.

As he pedalled home with the Tesco's madonna bumping up and down behind him, accusingly, Frank asked himself why on earth they did it; there was absolutely nothing in it for them.

Then he thought back to what Maggie had said, about him and Malcolm. If you pretended people were nice they just might end up improving, that's what she'd been getting at. All he could say was that they must have an awful lot of faith, to go on trying with thankless old men like Eric. Not that the old man was nasty to him, he seemed to like Frank, for some reason.

Outside their house something was going on which put the nuns and Eric right out of his head. He heard the voice before he saw anything, but he knew who it was straight away; Malc the Mok in full cry. He was dancing about on the pavement with a piece of paper in his hand, jerking his red crest up and down at somebody like an enraged parrot.

Frank climbed off his bike and began to push it slowly down Bailey Street. Three people stood arguing by the Renault 4; Slob, fatlegs Lesley, and a small dumpy figure in a navy mac. The familiar black and yellow hat told him everything. It was the newly appointed traffic warden.

'I don't bloody care,' he heard as he crept down the street. 'This is the second time you've done this to me, and I don't bloody like it.'

'Malcolm, for heaven's sake, keep your hair on, can't you? It's only a few quid and anyhow, you asked for it.' This was Lesley, trying to push him towards the open door of the Renault. She wasn't scared of Slob, in fact, now and again, she really told him off, and he took it. Today wasn't one of those days though. He shook her restraining hand off quite viciously, and went on bellowing at the traffic warden.

'I'm only doing my job, sir,' she was saying. 'I've already explained, I'd written the ticket out in full and that means it has to go through. If you want to make a formal complaint –'

'I *do*,' Malc bawled, 'and I *will*. Don't worry. I'll complain about *you*, coming round here with your fancy hat and your little roll of Sellotape. I'll tell you one thing,' he added as his parting shot, climbing into the car, 'they don't recruit women like you for your looks, do they?' and he started his engine.

'*Malcolm*,' Frank heard, as the door was slammed. 'There was no need to say that to her. That was awful.'

'Oh, dry up, you.'

As they rattled off up the street Lesley noticed Frank standing there and waved feebly, a look of pink embarrassment spreading across her plain, rather stupid face. Malc, who was obviously giving her a big lecture about sticking up for the traffic warden, spotted his brother staring at them and pulled the V sign.

Charming. What would Maggie think about that, then?

Outside their house there was a wall about two feet high with iron knobbles stuck into it where railings used to be. In the war they'd taken them away to melt down for guns. On one of the knobbles sat the offending traffic warden, huddled up and shaking with the tears rolling down her cheeks. As Frank drew level she blew her nose into a pink hanky.

'I'm really sorry,' he muttered. He'd got to say something.

'It's your brother, is it?' she sniffed, having another big blow. 'Thought it might be. I can see it in the face.'

Frank didn't like being identified with Slob but he couldn't blame her; everyone said they looked alike, even though Malc had gone punk and dyed his hair. He said, 'I don't know why he behaves like that. Something just gets into him and he flips his lid. I'm sure he'll pay up though, Lesley'll make him. She's his girlfriend. She says if he doesn't pull himself together and start behaving like a normal human being, she's going to chuck him, and he wouldn't like that.'

'It's nothing to me whether he pays up or not, love,' the traffic warden said. 'I'm just doing my job, that's all.'

'I really am sorry though,' Frank repeated. Malc should never have made that cruel remark about her appearance, but he could see why he'd said it. The squat, middle-aged woman who sat on the wall in a crumpled heap wouldn't exactly win a beauty contest. She had a faintly hairy face and a fine blonde moustache, and thick stubby legs encased in dark traffic-warden stockings. Her face was small yet it seemed to be all nose, and the nose was a bright pink now, from crying.

'That's all right; I've had worse. They warn you about this kind of thing, when they take you on. Anyhow, it's only a temporary job, till my insurance money comes through. I had to do something.'

She put the pink handkerchief back in a neat black shoulder bag, got to her feet and brushed her mac down.

But as she straightened her knees she began to sway about, made a grab at Frank and sat down again abruptly. 'Oh dear, I don't feel very well. I'm . . . this . . . it's all too much for me, this is,' and she started to cry again.

Alarmed, Frank looked up and down Bailey Street, then down at her. 'Listen, why don't you come inside for a minute?' he suggested kindly. If she fainted, out here on the pavement, she might get concussed, then the whole thing could turn into what newspapers called an 'official episode'. 'Love' was all very well, but he felt like killing Slob, reducing the poor woman to a shivering wreck and then just driving off.

'I'll make you a cup of tea, if you come inside,' he offered, holding on to her arm as she organized her Sellotape, her hat and her shoulder bag. 'Do you mind coming round the back, so I can put my bike in the shed?'

The woman was called Madge Shiplake and she knew Mr and Mrs Munn up the street. She didn't know Dad to speak to but she knew *of* him, and how he did little odd jobs for the Munns. She seemed quite at home by the gas-fire with the Flumps on her knee, and, now the colour was coming back to her face and she'd taken her official hat off, the all-nose face didn't look quite so grotesque. 'You make a very nice cup of tea, Frank,' she said, sipping appreciatively.

He wanted to know how anybody on this earth could have chosen to be a traffic warden. It was always in the paper, how angry motorists duffed them up. But she didn't seem inclined to go into details. All he could glean was that she was waiting for some whacking insurance payment. When it came she was going to buy her own business, Miss Sweeney, the ladies hairdresser's, which had been up for sale on South Parade, Denning. It was obviously her little dream to start up on her own. Frank understood entirely; he'd got dreams too.

'That's next to Wendy News, isn't it?' he said. Then

he added, with a touch of pride, 'I deliver newspapers for them.

'Our cat's having kittens,' he told her next.

'Is she? I'd quite like a cat myself,' she said, tickling Flump 1 behind the ears. 'They make a house a home, I always think.'

'That's what my dad says.'

'You see, it's something alive in the empty house, something waiting for you when you get back.'

In spite of the blonde moustache and the thick stumpy legs, Madge wore a thick gold wedding-ring. She'd been married, Frank decided, but was married no longer, and his hunch was that something awful must have happened to the husband. That was why she was getting some insurance money to buy Miss Sweeney. Only something as big as Death could have brought that terrible sadness into her face when she talked about her empty house.

'You could have one of our kittens,' he offered. 'She'll be having them soon. Should I put you down for one?'

'Er, well yes, that'd be nice. I'll certainly consider it anyway, and I'll let you know.'

'I've promised one to a friend of mine,' he explained, 'but you could have first pick. She's not bothered what hers looks like.' If Sister Geraldine agreed, Maggie was having one of the kittens for 105. They'd got mice.

'Have you started with girlfriends yet, Frank?' Madge said. 'You're a good-looking boy.'

Embarrassed, he fiddled with his hair. 'Ne'er, not really. There's someone I quite like but she's a bit old for me.'

Even if she wasn't she was already spoken for, he thought sadly, and the only other female he cared about was married to Jesus.

'Oh well, there's plenty of time, isn't there?'

She got up and swung the shoulder bag into position again. 'I'll go now, Frank. Thank you for the tea, and I'll be in touch about the kitten.'

'Ta, ta.'

He stood at the front door and watched her go up the street. Half-way along she stopped and stuck a ticket on an illegally parked Ford Fiesta. Well, she was only doing her job.

He'd not liked to say 'don't report my brother', it would have been too crude. He'd just have to pin his hopes on their cat agreement and on the fact that she'd said he made a good cup of tea. His instinct was that a homely woman like Madge Shiplake wouldn't bear grudges.

And he was right. When he put the milk bottles out that night he found an apple pie on the doorstep, wrapped in silver foil. 'From Madge' it said on the label, and it was still warm. She must have gone straight home and made it. Perhaps it was because he'd explained how Dad did most of the cooking now. Gran used to cook a lot and bring food down, but she couldn't do as much since her heart attack.

It was a pretty rotten pie though. He had a slice for his supper and it was like chewing wet cardboard. She'd forgotten to put the sugar in too. This was the kind of pie Moira Manning-Sanders would have made, if she'd actually approved of puddings.

It was a pity really. If only kindly Madge were a bit younger and prettier and a slightly better cook, he could have seen her getting along quite matey with Dad. As it was, romance seemed to be in the air. His father had spent hours in the bathroom that night; he'd hardly spoken to Frank.

Before going to bed, he took his usual peek in the back bedroom. Dad wasn't all bundled up in his normal fashion but lying flat on his back, very neatly arranged and completely symmetrical. His usually ruddy face was chalk white, as if it had been plastered with make-up.

Frank edged a bit nearer and stared down. *It had.* But the white wasn't make-up, it was some elaborate beauty preparation called 'Overnight Success', made from

101

essence of cucumbers. He could see the empty packet on the bedside table.

In his bid to find 'a sincere lady for a lasting relationship', his father was obviously sparing no expense. What next? A nightly chin-strap to reduce his double chin? Anti-wrinkle cream? A male corset?

Frank crept away to join Slob in the slum, not knowing whether to laugh or cry.

Chapter Eight

When she saw him on the Wednesday after the Sunday walk with Maggie, Lil at the paper shop said he could have a Sunday round. One of the Bryces' boys had gone off on a skiing trip without telling her, so she'd sacked him.

This bumped up his take-home pay quite nicely and the syrup tin where he kept his money grew heavier. He wasn't spending a penny of it though. In spite of the Wall Doctor's gloomy report and the green mould that was now creeping up the chimney-breast in the cellar, Frank still clung to his dream of making it into a cosy little den, like Tim's in Palace Road. All his Wendy News money was going towards that.

Spring was in the air and everyone except him seemed gripped by their own romantic projects. Flump 2 had turned very frisky and started sleeping away from home. Now the mother of his kittens was getting fat and slothful, he was obviously looking round for a replacement.

Frank was taking the pregnancy seriously. It didn't cost much; all the cat seemed to fancy beyond her normal diet was crispy bacon flavoured crisps. On Lesley's advice he'd prepared a special box for her to have the kittens in; a clean baked-beans carton he'd picked up at the supermarket and lined with an old blanket. 'Try and get her used to it,' Lesley had advised him. 'When they're ready to produce, cats can get into some funny

places; our Mutt had her last lot in the airing cupboard.'
So whenever Flump 1 started ranging about and looking
restless, he got her to lie down in her carton, and made
special reassuring noises.

A few days after the pie a fruit loaf was left on their
doorstep. It tasted faintly of boiled leather and the burnt
currants on top resembled rabbit droppings. With it
there was a little note from Madge to say she'd definitely
have a kitten and would five pounds be all right? Frank
was delighted. He'd not been expecting any money.

Dad's Lonelyhearts advert appeared twice in the *Spotlight* and through it he acquired a ladyfriend called Rita
Stone. She was a thin, ratty-looking woman with hard
blonde hair and she was always plastered with make-
up. Not Dad's usual type at all. Frank disliked her on
sight and Malc said she was 'bad news' too. It was the
first time the Tanner brothers had ever agreed on anything.

In spite of the 'two sons' bit in the advert, Rita wasn't
the least interested in Malcolm and Frank. When she
came round she never even took her coat off. Ten minutes in their sitting-room on the edge of her chair seemed
about as much as she could stomach of Tanner family
life, and she spent them chain-smoking and staring at
the telly, while Mr Tanner 'got ready'.

Where they actually went to, on their frequent evenings out, Frank couldn't discover. Dad never discussed
his friendship with Rita beyond saying that she was 'a
nice girl who'd had a rough time'. She was obviously
making up for it now though. The building society
accounts were definitely dwindling.

One night, Frank, Slob and Lesley discussed her in
private. Slob reckoned Rita Stone was taking his father
for a ride. 'She'll dump him in a few weeks,' he told
them. 'She's a little gold-digger, that's what she is.'

'Well, there's not much gold in this place,' Frank said
rather sadly, looking round the tatty little room. But in
his bones he knew his brother was right. 'Don't say

anything, Malc,' he pleaded. He couldn't bear another disappointment for Dad. Buying new clothes and shoes for his dates with Rita had really cheered him up, and the bathroom cabinet was steadily filling up with men's deodorants and lotions.

It was odd but since the Madge episode, Slob had become slightly more human. It must be because Lesley had threatened to chuck him if he didn't improve. There was a ring on her engagement finger now. It had only come off Darnley Market and it was rather cheap-looking, but she still displayed it proudly. On her fat finger it looked like a Christmas-cracker ring garnishing a sausage.

They were busy making their own plans, saving up for a meal at the Manor Hotel in Cavendish. It was the best eating place in the area and you didn't get much change from eighty pounds, for a candlelit dinner for two. The meal was to 'celebrate'. From now till then Lesley was dieting so she could pig out on the big night. They were even talking of growing their hairdos out. They didn't want to get turned away. Slob had already bought matching designer trousers and shirt to wear. Frank had seen them in his drawer and the price tags were beyond belief.

'Celebrate' what though? Engagement rings were a bit old-fashioned but they meant wedding bells, didn't they? It'd be great if it meant Malcolm moving out of the front bedroom. That would be the perfect answer to the mould and frogs problem down in the cellar. Frank wasn't banking on it though. Things you pinned your biggest hopes on had a nasty habit of falling flat.

Twice a week in class Miss Halliwell was letting them do their projects, and his was getting quite thick. He'd been working steadily through all the back numbers, filling out his special sections with dramatic items about chip-pan fires, toddlers' thumbs getting jammed in taps, and thefts of microwave ovens. Those cuttings had gone into his 'Man with the Birthmark' envelope. He'd not had any more sightings though.

He'd been right about Madge's husband. In last November 10th's *Examiner* he found a piece about a fire that had raged through a slipper factory in Oldham. A Mr 'Jimmy' Shiplake, an employee of Bates Brothers for thirty-six years, had been trapped in a basement store-room and burned to death. Identification of the body had been made from dental records.

Poor Madge. But at least she'd been spared what they were always showing you on telly, a doctor lifting up a sheet to expose a dead face and the relation looking down at it, then passing out from the shock. A kitten wouldn't do much to replace Madge's Jimmy but, now he knew about the fire, Frank was determined to keep a very strict eye on Flump 1. Mrs Shiplake was going to be presented with the healthiest kitten in Darnley.

During the project lessons Tim Manning-Sanders always got very depressed. Frank couldn't understand it. Everything he'd written so far had been beautifully typed out and there were coloured photographs on every single page. All the notes were kept in a smart black ring-file with his name and form blocked on the spine in gold. Why was Frank bothering to compete? Tim had more or less won already.

It was obviously his mother. 'She keeps nagging me about it,' he told Frank one afternoon. 'What she really wants is for me to go into the E form and she thinks they'd move me, if I won a prize.'

'Don't you like being in our form then? H for Hope-less?' He probably shouldn't have said that but moany Tim sometimes got on his nerves a bit. He ought to try having real troubles, a father that wore nightly facepacks to attract scheming women, sweaty Malcolm as a room-mate and frogs in the cellar.

Tim blushed. 'Course I don't. It's just *her*. Your project looks good anyhow, Frank,' he said timidly. 'I told Cass what you were doing and she thought it sounded fantastic.'

Ah yes, Cass. Frank had only been up to their house once, since he'd seen her at the Stones with that boy. Barry Townsend he was called and he sometimes waited for her now, outside the school gates. She always said hello to Frank, when she saw him, and waved cheerily. That made it all worse.

When he didn't reply, Tim tried another tack. He said, 'Did your father get the loan?'

'Not yet. They're still thinking about it.' He wasn't letting on that Dad had been turned down flat and that he now had quite a thick file of letters from Mr Brocklehurst at the bank about his application, in the sideboard drawer. Frank had read them all through one night in private, and it was obvious that his father was starting to annoy the Shorrock Street bank manager, with his string of complaining letters and his repeated requests for the loan to be 'reconsidered'. He was getting obsessed.

'I could have a word with my father, if you like,' Tim offered, 'and he could speak to the man at your dad's branch. I don't understand why they're being so slow, you owning a big house in Baillie Terrace and everything.'

'*No*,' Frank said, rather louder than he'd intended. 'Please don't say anything, my father wouldn't like it. He'll wait. It's OK.'

Yet another white lie was catching up with him. Little deceits multiplied and thickened, like the mossy green patches on their cellar wall.

He'd only done his Sunday round twice when something happened that threatened to end his job with Wendy News for ever. Another old lady was beaten up and robbed on the Larkfield Estate.

Dad immediately decided that doing an early-morning paper round was too risky. 'If you really want to carry on with it,' he said, 'I'd better come with you. I could use our Malcolm's bike, it only needs oiling.'

'*No*,' Frank protested. 'You can't come trailing round after me, Dad, people would laugh. Anyhow, that old lady's going to be OK. She's recovering in Darnley Infirmary.'

'That's not the point,' Mr Tanner said. 'There are some terrible people around these days. I'm worried about you.'

He'd have been a lot more worried if he'd known that Frank had actually been to look at the scene of the crime. It had happened on Rawlinson Road, only a couple of streets away from Lime Walk; he and Tim had gone over there, the day it had happened.

They'd found a crowd of people on the pavement, watching a couple of policemen at work in the little front garden. Portions of it had been cordoned off with white tape. One man was taking measurements and the other dusting the paintwork for fingerprints. A third was talking to people in the crowd, and taking notes. One of them was the man with the birthmark.

Frank watched him very closely as he stood answering the policeman's questions. He seemed quite relaxed and he actually cracked a joke or two. Frank edged nearer, to try to catch what they were saying, and he heard him give the man in uniform an address. '10 Nelson Street,' he said. 'You know, it's over Cavendish way. Well, let me know if I can be of any more help,' and he was off, jogging athletically down Rawlinson Road, a small, neat man, a man in control. He'd seen Frank standing with Tim in the crowd, but there'd not been the least glimmer of recognition.

Nelson Street, Cavendish. Frank brooded about it all the way home. He was probably 'romancing' again but he wasn't quite satisfied. Foxy, he'd decided, definitely wasn't the Larkfield Killer. He'd had a closer look at those identikit pictures now. There wasn't really any resemblance at all, and no mention of a birthmark. But if Larkfield and Denning were his 'patch', an area he dipped into now and again to supplement his income, it'd actually be quite a clever move to seem *co-operative* with the police, a good way of deflecting suspicion when his next bit of thieving hit the headlines.

Nelson Street could easily be a false address. Frank rummaged through his brain and examined his collection of telly plots. What you did, if the police got too keen, was to give the address of a mate, someone who'd say, 'Oh yes, he did live here, but he moved out last month and I don't know where he's gone.' Alternatively, Foxy could have supplied the address of an ex-girlfriend – his old mum, even. But what about 49 Lime Walk? He'd definitely gone in there.

That same night Frank had slipped out and gone spying. He'd been in luck this time because the front curtains at 49 hadn't been drawn properly. Holding his breath, and trembling at the mere cheek of it, he'd knelt down in the damp grass underneath the window and peeped through the narrow triangle of light.

He had seen a small narrow room that ran front to back, extremely neat but very skimpily furnished. Everything was cheap and ugly-looking; easy chairs whose scratched wooden arms and black plastic seats looked anything but 'easy', a small faded piece of carpet on top of cracked lino, and a decrepit bookcase full of paperbacks in one corner. The only other thing in the room was a TV set and the man with the birthmark sat in front of it, drinking a can of beer.

As Frank crouched outside he heard a noise coming from an upstairs room. 'Dad . . . *Dad* . . . ' a child's voice whimpered. 'I want a drink.' The minute he heard it, the man put his beer down on the floor, switched the sound off and went out of the room.

There was nothing else to see and he couldn't trust his luck too far, so he crept back down the garden and pedalled home. Foxy had kids then. But where was the mother? The comfortless room hadn't suggested that anyone else was around, to make things nice.

The thought of that miserable plastic interior depressed him. Bailey Street was nothing special, yet Dad had a homely touch with things around the house. He'd got plants on the kitchen window-sill and a bright rug in front of the gas-fire that really cheered the place up. It was what you did with the bits and pieces you had that made the difference.

It occurred to Frank that 10 Nelson Street might be where the wife lived. Half the kids in his class had parents who lived apart. Why give that address to the police though? They'd track him down in the end, if they really needed to.

When he'd got home he'd pulled down Dad's *A–Z of Greater Manchester* from the top shelf of the oak book-case in the front room. It was a collection of streetmaps and Darnley-in-Makerfield was included.

He spent ages poring over it, checking and re-checking, to make sure he'd not misheard. There were five Nelson Streets listed, two in Manchester itself, one in Oldham, one in Bacup and one in Rochdale. But there was definitely nothing listed under Cavendish, Darnley.

So, unless he'd made a mistake, and he'd not, the man with the red hair and the birthmark had – for his own curious reasons – supplied the police with a *false address*.

Less than a week after the mugging on Rawlinson Road, the Manning-Sanderses got burgled. It was a Friday, and Frank had been planning to go to the Safari Launderette for Dad. Rita Stone had taken him shopping in Manchester and another fifty quid had disappeared from his Leeds account.

The phone had rung just as he was getting the dirty washing together. It was Moira, asking him to go up to Palace Road. 'You probably won't know what's happened exactly, Frank,' she said. 'I told Tim to keep quiet about it at school. The less people know at this stage the

110

better. The thing is, we've had a break-in and some of our neighbours are coming round this evening, to discuss general strategy; I'd rather like you to be there.'

'But why me?' It was as if she thought he'd got something to do with the robbery. Why rope him in? 'I'm busy tonight,' he said cautiously. 'I've got to go to the launderette, for my Dad.'

'The *launderette*? Don't you have a washing machine?'

'Oh yes,' he lied. 'Course we do. Only, it's broken.'

'Well, it's only five o'clock, Frank,' she said briskly, 'and we're not starting till seven-thirty. I'd like you to be there because you're up at odd hours, doing your deliveries. You could collect some very useful information for us. Coffee and cake after the meeting,' she added winningly, obviously hoping to tempt him.

Well, coffee gave him wind and he didn't fancy Moira's carrot cake. But he wasn't doing anything else and Maggie might have been invited. He'd not seen her all week; she'd been over in Leeds at their 'Mother Convent'.

'OK,' he said grudgingly. 'I don't see how I can help though.'

'Oh, you'd be surprised,' she said, gushing a bit now. 'See you at seven-thirty. Have fun at the laundromat.'

He put the phone down, went into the kitchen and started stuffing the laundry into two big plastic carriers. *Have fun* . . . it was all right for her.

As he trudged along the streets he kept his eyes skinned for Flump 1. She'd disappeared early that morning and he was worried. Lesley had said the cat would have her kittens any time now and in the last few days she'd become restless. He kept finding her in silly places, first on top of Dad's wardrobe, then under his bed, then trying to get comfortable on a pile of old newspapers out in the shed. The one place she refused to consider was Frank's carefully prepared baked-beans carton.

There was no sign of her on Bailey Street and once he'd crossed Rochdale Road he gave up looking. Flump 1

111

had always kept to her own little patch, unlike Flump 2 who'd definitely gone off the rails and was now painting the town red every night.

The only animal he saw between home and the launderette was an obese black tom sitting outside Dad's branch of the Friendly Northern Bank on Shorrock Street. It looked like a bank cat, smug and self-satisfied, and Frank pulled a mental tongue out at it as he walked past. The man in that hut was responsible for his father's depression. One stroke of his pen could transform Mr Tanner's whole world. But big people in banks didn't seem to think about all the little people, waiting hopefully at home for the vital letter, the letter that said 'yes'.

Frank had a shock when he reached the launderette. There was a blue motor bike parked outside, its white carrier plastered with coloured stickers, Spot the Dog, Superman and My Little Pony. In a daze he elbowed the door open and went in. There, on an orange plastic chair, sat the man with the birthmark, watching his washing through a soapy porthole. Behind him, on the wall, a string of grotesquely yellow camels trailed across a peeling desert towards a luminous green oasis.

The Safari Launderette was long and narrow with a table down the middle where people could sort their stuff out. Frank stationed himself directly opposite Foxy's chair, emptied his bags and started separating coloureds from whites.

The smell was embarrassing and it was all due to Slob's socks; stale cat-food, cabbage, mixed with a touch of sick, just about summed it up. Malcolm spent quite a bit of money on clothes, sixty quid for example on the designer gear he'd bought for their celebration meal at the Manor. But socks and underwear came low on his list of priorities and he didn't change them often enough, in spite of Lesley's nagging. The result was that his dirty washing could have hopped off that table and jumped into the nearest machine all by itself.

When the clothes were installed in two washers and

were going through their main cycle, Frank sat down opposite Foxy, took a comic from his anorak and pretended to read. But all the time he kept checking up on what the man with the birthmark was doing.

After a few minutes he decided to try one of his special stares. Foxy was taking no notice of him at all, but Frank was determined to get his attention. If he was going to pursue this notion of his being an unofficial supply man for shops like Merrick's, and the idea interested him, then he ought to establish whether he remembered that day on Larkfield, when he'd caught him checking out the Morris Minor with the piece of bent wire.

So he stared, so hard and long that his eyes began to feel bulgy and sore. The man didn't react at first, then he started to fidget, pulling at his shirt collar and straightening the front of his jacket, looking down at his unexceptionable clothes then staring back at Frank with a questioning, almost apologetic look.

Then he glanced past him to one of the two washers, and said casually, 'I think you're in trouble there, mate. It looks as if something's running.'

Frank got up and inspected his machines. His coloureds looked harmless enough but his whites were in dead trouble. As the steel drum stopped in mid-cycle, made a faint creaking noise then started to rotate the other way, he thrust his face up against the glass porthole. The washing water had turned bright pink and all the clothes had gone a sickly rose colour. As the technicoloured bubbles began swishing over them again he could see the offending articles quite clearly, two bright red socks that belonged to Malc. Lesley had presented them to him only last week, in the hope that he'd get the big idea about his sweaty feet. They must have got inside one of the pillowcases.

'Oh *heck*,' he muttered, staring helplessly at the washing machine. 'My father's best shirt's in there, and all his underwear as well.' Dad probably wouldn't mind

113

wearing pale pink Y-fronts but the shirt was very bad news. It was a recent buy for his dates with Rita.

'Use some bleach on it when you get home,' Foxy suggested helpfully.

'But can't we stop the machine?' Frank said, forgetting that this was the man with the birthmark, the man who'd got an envelope all to himself. All that pink froth was making him panic now.

'No point, mate, the damage is done. Anyhow, it'll have to go through its cycle. Red's a terrible colour for running; I once put a little red skirt of our Jackie's in with some whites and it ruined them.'

But Frank was too agitated to wonder who 'our Jackie' might be. He'd seen something else in the washing machine, a definite foreign body. Swishing quietly round with Slob's luminous socks and Dad's pink Y-fronts, he'd spotted what looked like a photograph.

When the drum creaked to a halt again he hunched closer and pressed his nose against the warm glass. He could see it quite clearly now in the bottom of the door. It was that holiday snap of Cass he'd nicked from Tim's bedroom. It must somehow have fallen through the bottom of the Put-U-Up, where he'd hidden it, and got swept up with the washing.

He straightened up, sat down again, and eyed the whirling machine with real hate. He felt like giving it a good kick. Somehow, what it had done to the precious photograph summed up what was happening to his life in general.

The gorgeous Cass, on holiday in Spain, now resembled a bright pink pig: pink cheeks, pink eyes, pink hair, and behind her a pink church and a pink sun. And because the machine had creased the photo right across the middle, her gentle smile had turned into rather a nasty leer. By the time it had done its final rinse she'd resemble a vampire, drooling blood.

Frank turned away and concentrated on Foxy who

was now loading his wash into a yellow basket. That photo had become a mockery of all his hopes.

'Do you really think bleach'll get it out?' he said, actually helping to disentangle a pair of tiny trousers from a man's shirt.

'Should do, if you soak it the minute you get home.'

Frank watched him tip the clothes into a dryer. Apart from the odd shirt and a pair of jeans, the whole wash consisted of child's clothing, obviously a little girl's. Everything was spotted or frilly, or patterned with teddy bears. 'Our Jackie' had quite an extensive wardrobe.

He walked home miserably, lugging his pink whites, his eyes still skinned for Flump 1. At least, now, he could put his 'Foxy file' away. The man with the birthmark was obviously harmless, just a single parent who'd been left on his own to look after his little girl. The mother had walked out, presumably, unless she'd died, like his. He must have made a mistake about '10 Nelson Street', or there must be a simple explanation. All those suspicious bits and pieces about Foxy had never added up to much anyhow. They were just fabrications, things he'd dredged up from nothing to give his rather boring life a bit of excitement and colour.

Barry Townsend at the Nine Standards had been real enough though, wearing his black glasses and holding hands with Cassie. As he turned the last corner into Bailey Street Frank stopped, tore up the grinning pink photo into tiny pieces, and fed them through the bars of a grid. That was over too.

Dad used bleach for the lavatory and he found half a bottle under the sink. He filled the bath with cold water, emptied some of it in, then tipped the pink whites in, swishing them round. By the time he got back from Palace Road he hoped something would have happened. It was a good job Dad wasn't getting back till late though; the bleach had made the whole house smell like Darnley Public Baths.

115

In the kitchen he spooned food out for the two cats. Flump 2 ate his in seconds then polished the other bowl off too before Frank could put it out of reach. Still no sign of Flump 1. He checked all round once again, before going to get his bike out, and he kept his eyes open all across Larkfield too.

What he dreaded most was finding a little furry corpse squashed flat on that dual carriageway. Cats could travel miles if the mood took them, and according to Lesley 'moods' went with pregnancy. But though he looked very carefully there was no sign of the little cat, living or dead. He'd just got to be realistic, and tell himself that 'no news was good news'.

Chapter Nine

'I hope nobody minds sitting in the kitchen,' Tim's mother said. 'The drawing-room's larger but I think we need a table.'

Frank sat between Tim and Cassie, unnerved by the navy-blue presence of a police officer only three seats away. What if he asked about the picture that had disappeared from next door?

'Don't know why we had to come,' Tim grumbled to him, as his mother produced a sheaf of papers from a briefcase. 'I notice my dad's not here. It was neat of him to stay in Paris, at his conference.'

'Mum wants moral support,' Cassie whispered. 'I think she's frightened of Dr Piggott,' and she giggled.

Frank couldn't really imagine Moira Manning-Sanders being frightened of anyone, the way she went briskly round the table, asking everyone present to give their names and addresses. He immediately forgot most of the names but there was no forgetting Lilian Piggott. She was that woman with the bust who lived in the No Anything house on Victoria Avenue.

The minute she saw Frank she called out, 'I've seen you before, haven't I? Didn't you once leave me a free newspaper *when I expressly told you not to*?' She pronounced the last bit as if it was written in dripping red capital letters, and glared across the table.

'Oh, but we *love* the free papers, Dr Piggott,' someone

said enthusiastically, and a familiar face peeped round the bust. It was Maggie. 'You can get some fantastic bargains out of the classified section, you know,' she added helpfully.

'I'm referring to the fact that this boy –'

'And Frank's a real help to us in 105. He's wonderful with the elderly, you know, our old men love him . . .'

Clever Maggie, to have turned up at this meeting. The idea behind it, as Moira was now explaining, was to organize the neighbours into keeping an eye on each other's houses, a 'neighbourhood watch scheme' it was called. Police Constable Jefferson had only come to the meeting as an 'observer'. But the police would help them all they could. Frank knew that Tim's mother was against the nuns, because of the way they 'encouraged' the old men. But if they co-operated in this scheme, she'd have to be nice to them.

When she'd explained what she wanted everyone to do, things like keeping your immediate neighbours informed about holidays, not leaving milk bottles uncollected on steps, or newspapers sticking out of letterboxes, she passed round copies of some information that had been supplied by the police constable. They detailed all the break-ins which they'd been called to in the Denning area in the last six months, and they listed times, places and objects stolen.

Frank ran his eye down the computer-printed sheet with a certain satisfaction. He knew all this already; it was neatly written up in his 'Man with the Birthmark' envelope, this curious string of petty thefts that didn't really make economic sense. Nobody was going to get rich from nicking what was listed here – portable radios, toasters, personal stereo sets and money – when people had been daft enough to leave it lying around.

What he hadn't known till now was what precisely had disappeared in the Manning-Sanders burglary. When he found the answer, the most recent item on the list, he couldn't really understand what Moira was making such a fuss about. All they'd lost was their video recorder and a few old books. He'd expected a new Porsche at the very least.

'We mark our valuables with a special security kit,' she was saying, holding up a blue plastic package. 'This contains all you need to do the job and costs less than ten pounds. The electronic needle is used to mark a number on the item in question and, once marked, such a number isn't easily removed, is it, Constable Jefferson? So if the item should turn up for sale, in a shop, for example, it's easily identified. Any number will do but we used my husband's birthday, 17-10-44. So if anybody is offered a second-hand video recorder with that number on it, I'd be most grateful to be told.'

'And the books?' Dr Piggott said, writing down the magic number. (Frank, who forgot most things, would remember that in his head because it happened to be Dad's birthday too.)

'Well, this is interesting, Lilian. They were quite valuable as it happens, a set of early Beatrix Potters in their original wooden case. They were on top of the video machine because Cassandra was supposed to be finding a place for them, up in her bedroom. Her godmother gave them to her, when she was a baby. We treasured them.'

'So it's possible that whoever took them also took Sister Mary Magdalen's Italian miniature the other week? Hmm, I think we may have a very discriminating thief here,' and Dr Piggott pulled her mouth about and studied the police list with ferocious intensity.

Frank didn't dare look up but he could feel his face burning. Officially, it was only girls that blushed, teenage girls and women of Moira's vintage. But he could feel the red starting in his neck, spreading up into his cheeks and past them to his hairline. His heart was thumping so violently Cassie must surely be able to hear it too, and his hot damp hands were twisted together in a sweaty knot under the table.

'Well, possibly, but the real point is this: the law can only do so much, as you've already heard from the police constable. If we want to live here in Denning without the constant threat of our homes being ransacked by these miserable pilferers, we must all keep our wits about us, and our eyes and ears open. To this end,' she went on rather grandly, 'I'd be willing to offer money for information. Everybody needs money these days, especially youngsters. You'll have noticed that I asked my own children to be present this evening, and their friend Frank Tanner. Frank earns extra pocket money by delivering papers in this area but he actually lives in the town centre, in Baillie Terrace. That's another part of the town favoured by these light-fingered friends of ours, or so the police tell me.'

There she went again. Frank should have told her, when she first made the mistake, that Baillie Terrace and Bailey Street were as different as chalk from cheese. If only he'd explained at the beginning. Lies had a habit of catching up with you and it *was* a kind of lie, letting her make that big mistake.

When the coffee and cake were produced, the meeting turned into a general chat. Frank decided to skip the refreshments in case Moira trapped him into an awkward conversation about the high life of Baillie Terrace, but she bore down on him before he reached the door, with a slice of iced-carrot special on a plate. 'If you could keep your eyes open, Frank,' she said, 'I really would be most grateful. And it might earn you a little money.'

'What sort of information do you want, exactly?' he asked her.

'Anything out of the ordinary. The point is, you deliver your papers at roughly the same time each morning, don't you?'

'Yes. Only three times a week though.'

'It doesn't matter, we're all creatures of habit, Frank. We tend to do the same things at the same time, each day. Something even very slightly unusual would stick out a mile, wouldn't it – if you were an observant individual. And I'm sure you are.'

'Like that motor bike,' Dr Piggott said, barging forwards and edging Frank sideways with her bust.

'What motor bike?'

'*Which* motor bike, Frank, *which*,' Mrs Manning-Sanders corrected smoothly. 'Somebody left a motor bike on Dr Piggott's property.'

'I have an extra piece of garden, separate from the house,' she told him. 'I'm planning to grow vegetables on it. This machine was left there for several hours the other evening, dripping oil all over the place. Disgusting. I went out several times to see if it had gone. One last check,' I told myself, 'and I'll ring the police. But it had been removed, mercifully.'

'I don't suppose you got the number, did you?' Frank said, starting to feel slightly peculiar, 'or the make?'

'Unfortunately, no. It was a blue machine, quite large. That's all I can remember, I'm afraid.'

'That's what I mean, Frank,' Moira said, almost gleeful. 'No doubt the motor bike wouldn't have led to anything in itself, but it's the kind of thing we need to watch out for. Now, if you'd just take these, and give them to friends you think might be interested. There could be fifty pounds in it for someone coming up with some hard information. The video recorder doesn't matter in itself, the insurance will more than cover that, but I do rather want Cassie's Beatrix Potters back. And, of course, it's all the other nasty little thefts we need information on. It's the principle of the thing that concerns me.'

Frank took the police lists, rolled them up and stuck them inside his jacket. Mentally, he'd closed his 'Man with the Birthmark' file an hour or so ago, in the Safari Launderette. Now, though he didn't much want to, he could see he might have to open it again. The blue motor bike had got to be Foxy's.

'I've just been telling Miss Pearson here about Eric's

121

trip to Blackpool,' Maggie said, coming up and tucking her arm through his. 'We've got him a lovely suit by the way, we found it in some jumble. I was saying that you'll have to persuade him to wear it, on the day. This boy's got a real knack with old people, Mrs Manning-Sanders. He's marvellous.'

'I'm sure he is,' Tim's mother said, but flatly, as if she'd not really heard. She was much too taken up with her new scheme to think about next-door's tramps.

As he was going down the hall, Cassie popped her head round the kitchen door and shouted, 'Why don't you stay on for a bit, Frank? Barry's coming over in a few minutes and we are all going down to South Parade for fish and chips. We always do, on Fridays. It's my mother's night off.' She was still as friendly as ever.

'Er, no thanks,' he said. 'I've got to get back. See you,' and he went off down the path, not even looking round as he shut the gate behind him. He was quite satisfied now that Cass really didn't know what he'd begun to feel for her, deep inside, how she was one of the beautiful things he needed in his life. If she did, she surely couldn't be rubbing salt in his wound now, by suggesting he went down for chips with her and Barry and Tim.

She would certainly have understood though if she'd seen him tearing up the pink pig photo, and feeding it down the bars of the gutter at the bottom of their street.

It felt funny at home, partly because it was Friday and the Tanners had their weekly rituals too. There was no Dad tonight though, peacefully going through his newspapers for electrical bargains, and no box of meringues on the table. Malc was out, according to his usual Friday night pattern, but things still didn't feel right. Frank was lonely.

He switched the gas-fire on, then telly, and sat aimlessly watching, chewing on a rock cake. Madge had left some on the step, while he was out. His theory was that she was too timid to knock on the door; he reckoned she hung about till she was sure the house was empty, then crept up with her offerings.

It was a good job Miss Sweeney's was a hairdresser's, not a bakery, because the rock cakes were living up to their name. Frank had to go very carefully in case he loosened his fillings. It was a pity Madge was so shy, he reflected, as he lobbed what he couldn't eat into the waste-paper basket. He could have done with someone to talk to tonight. And she might know what the next stage should be with the pink whites. Everything in the bath was a dirty coffee colour now.

When the phone rang he picked it up rather edgily. Normally, he didn't mind being on his own in the house, it was just tonight. Perhaps it was Moira's burglary meeting and all that fierce talk of hers about 'suspicious and dangerous-looking individuals'. He'd be quite relieved when Dad came home.

But it was Dad on the telephone, ringing to say that he was stuck in Manchester. 'There's a long gap now, before the next bus,' he explained. 'So don't stay up.'

'How late are you going to be then? Will you be taking Rita home first?' She lived on the other side of Darnley, so walking her home would add another hour on.

There was a slight pause, then his father said, 'Er, no. I'll be coming straight home tonight.' His voice sounded defeated, almost crushed, and Frank was immediately suspicious. Rita Stone must have gone off earlier, on her own.

'Is everything OK, Dad?'

'Yes, perfectly all right, son. We've had a nice little evening. Was there any second post?'

'No.'

'So there's nothing more from the bank?'

'No.'

'OK then. I should be back about quarter to midnight. Leave the hall light on.'

'Er, Dad, I had a little accident at the launderette. Your new white shirt's gone a bit pink.'

123

'Not the one I got last week?'

'Yeah. Listen, I'm sorry, Dad.'

Another long pause then, 'I – oh well, it's only a shirt. Listen, soak it in cold water. Don't use bleach or anything, that'll ruin it.'

Oh heck. 'I really am sorry, Dad,' he said aloud. 'It was one of our Malcolm's socks. It ran.'

They were cut off then, and not a minute too soon, for Frank. Dad had said 'only a shirt' but he'd sounded positively wounded. His reaction was nothing to do with the shirt turning pink, Frank decided; it was because of Rita Stone. Their 'sincere relationship' couldn't be working out right.

One part of him was glad. He didn't like ratty Rita at all. Yet his heart ached for his father whose little round face had been bright with hope that morning as he'd made his careful plans for the trip to Manchester.

He'd got his Saturday paper round tomorrow morning, so he may as well go to bed. The last thing he did was to let Flump 2 out into the backyard. The little cat darted joyously through his legs and was gone. It was the last Frank would see of him tonight. He'd be back tomorrow though, stuffing himself with Go-Cat before settling down for a day's kip in the baked-beans carton. It was his now. Still no sign of Flump 1, even though Frank called for ages. In the end he closed the back door again, put the sneck down on the Yale lock, slid the bolts top and bottom and went up to bed.

He'd been meaning to tidy the room up tonight but he felt too tired now. He got into his pyjamas by the light of the bedside lamp. The main bulb, which had no proper shade, was too strong and glaring and it showed the room up in all its squalor. But he had no heart for spring-cleaning this evening.

He was getting himself comfortable in Malc's bed when he heard a funny noise on the other side of the room, a thin cheeping sound that seemed to be coming out of the chest-of-drawers. His first thought was mice,

124

but they'd never been troubled with those in Bailey Street. They'd got spiders under the beds and frogs in the cellar but not mice. There was a first time for everything though.

He got up, padded across the floor and listened very carefully. There it was again, and now he was closer it was more distinct, a little chirrupy noise, a little song of triumph.

Then he knew. 'Puss,' he said softly. 'Puss.' He always called that at the back door; 'Flump 1' sounded too daft. And out of the top left-hand drawer, which Slob had left half open, as usual, popped a little grey head and a pair of little grey ears, cocked and bristling, in case danger threatened. Everything was different now. She was a mother.

Oh, cat. Frank put his hand on the round wooden knob, then took it away again. If she'd really had her kittens, and she had – he could see two little squirmy things wriggling helplessly underneath her – it was vital that she was left severely alone. According to Lesley, if you interfered the mother might go funny. She might abandon the kittens, or attack them, or even try to eat them. Animals, like human beings, sometimes suffered from the post-baby blues.

Frank switched the main light on, then peered into the drawer. He expected a real mess, blood and guts and pink jelly, a repetition of that live human birth they'd seen on the school telly, but shrunk down in scale. There was quite a bit of gunge in there, but not nearly as much as he'd feared. Nature was wonderful, Lesley had told him, and the mother cat usually ate a lot of the debris, to keep her strength up. She wasn't eating it now though, she was licking the two squirmy pink babies all over. After a minute, she poked her head out and licked at Frank's finger too with her rough little tongue. It felt great, as if she was sharing all this with him, this birth, the biggest event of her life.

Dreamily, he went back to bed and lay there for a bit,

just thinking. Two perfect kittens, definitely alive and both sucking away for dear life. And the mother still in one piece after her ordeal, positively chirpy in fact. He was doing absolutely nothing till tomorrow, then he'd have to organize litter trays and things. For now, she could use the newspaper he'd spread out on the floor, and the kittens would obviously have to use Slob's drawer. You couldn't expect them to be potty-trained at their age.

Slob's drawer! In the middle of his fatherly meditations, Frank had a sudden sickening thought. He got out of bed again, switched the light on and inspected its contents. The cat bobbed up, reproachfully this time. Dark meant sleep and she'd just got her babies comfortable. What was he doing, switching the light on and interfering?

He was interfering because she'd given birth to her kittens on top of Malcolm's designer clothes, the ones he'd bought for his celebration meal at the Manor Hotel. Even though she'd obviously cleaned up after the birth, there were some suspicious stains on the clothing underneath the sleeping kittens. 'Peter and Paul of Wilmslow' he read on a label, '15½" collar'. But the pale green shirt and the dark green jeans would never be quite the same again.

He had hoped, after discovering Nature's miracle in the top left-hand drawer, to drift off peacefully, dreaming about the mystery of new life. As it was, he lay awake for hours worrying, and when he did fall asleep he dreamt of Slob, and of Peter and Paul from Wilmslow, all screaming at him and hacking him to death with machetes.

It was the beginning of what went down in Frank's personal history as the Black Weekend.

Chapter Ten

For a start, Dad was no help at all about the new babies. When Frank got back from his paper round next morning, he was already up and dressed, and reading a letter. He was so absorbed in it that he hardly reacted when he heard that the kittens had arrived. The bank had sent its very last refusal.

'They say it's their last word,' he said bleakly, as Frank walked in and hung his orange and banana delivery bag behind the kitchen door. 'So I'm going to talk to your Uncle Phil this morning, to see what he advises.'

'Dad, it's *useless.*' 'Uncle' Phil Cunningham was a solicitor in Rochdale. He'd been at school with Mr Tanner and they'd 'kept up' ever since.

'It's the principle of the thing, Frank. I don't see why I should lie down under shabby treatment like this.'

'What "principle"?' He had a sneaking feeling that his father didn't know.

'I've not got time to discuss it just at this moment. It's not the money; I can shelve that little project. There are other ways of making a living. It's just that, well, I won't be treated like dirt. I've had enough of it.'

Mr Tanner was near to tears and his voice wobbled as he did his coat up. Frank glanced at him as he stood in front of the kitchen mirror, tidying the scant remains of his hair with a little comb. He wanted to give him a big hug and tell him he was a great Dad, but this definitely wasn't the right moment.

'I'll be out most of the day, but I'll keep in touch.'

'What are you doing then, after you've been to Rochdale?' Frank didn't much want to be left on his own to face Malcolm. He needed moral support, over the kittens.

'I'm going to see Rita. We've got things to talk about.'

So his hunch had been right. Something funny had happened last night. If she was going to give Dad the push, Frank just hoped she'd be nice about it. He had a distinct feeling that he was at the end of his tether with life in general.

'What about the cats, and that mess on our Malcolm's new gear?' he called out, as his father opened the front door.

'I've already told you, I'll sort it out with him tonight. Tell him from me that he's not to touch them on any account. Those are my strict orders. OK?'

'Strict orders' were less than useless, so far as his brother was concerned, and Frank went back to sit by the gas-fire feeling very resentful. Malcolm paid little enough attention to his father's wishes when he was there in the flesh. Leaving instructions with his kid brother would achieve precisely nothing.

The minute he showed up, with Lesley in tow and Kentucky Fried Chicken in a carrier for their dinners, Frank took a deep breath and explained about Flump 1 having her kittens in his drawer. 'But it's OK, Malcolm, honestly,' he reassured him. 'I'm sure your stuff'll be all right. It just needs sponging.'

But Slob didn't wait to hear any more. He pushed his chicken legs to one side, shoved his brother out of the way and headed for the stairs.

'Malcolm!' Frank yelled after him, 'don't touch them, *please*. It's dangerous, she might eat them. Listen, I'll pay for the stuff if you want.'

If he did it would be the end of his cellar conversion

scheme. It'd take him weeks to save up the money for new clothes from Peter and Paul of Wilmslow. Better that, though, than have something awful happen to those two kittens. He'd knelt by the drawer for ages this morning, just watching. It was marvellous how Flump 1 knew exactly what to do. She was only a scrap of a thing herself and yet somehow the birth had made her much older, much more dignified. That's what mother-love did for people.

'*Lesley*,' Frank said in desperation, as he heard Slob banging about upstairs. 'Talk to him . . . don't let him touch them . . .' But she didn't need telling. Her fat legs had already wobbled off into the hall and he could hear her lumbering up the stairs.

After a few seconds' quiet a slanging match started up, over his head, Malc opening his big mouth and yelling, as usual, and Lesley yelling back. Their voices were muffled but it was quite obvious that she wasn't caving in. The thumps and bumps through the ceiling got steadily louder, punctuated by the odd roar from Malc and an occasional squeal from Lesley. Frank sat listening by the gas-fire, his head filled with a vision of two Sumo wrestlers heaving themselves about on the upstairs lino. Who was going to come off best? Malcolm was wiry and tough but Lesley was a very big girl.

Suddenly there was a crash and he heard '*Malcolm!*' A real scream it was, followed by a series of yelps and a pummelling noise. 'Leave off, leave *off*, you're breaking my collar bone. Listen, it's only a bleedin' cat. You're mad, you are.' Frank heard that bit quite clearly and from the noises off he deduced that they were now heading for the stairs, still locked in combat.

But before he saw them he saw Flump 1. She shot through from the hall, streaked across the sitting-room and leaped through the back door which had blown open, as usual. He ran to the kitchen window and saw her scramble up the gate, run along the wall and disappear. Seconds later he was outside himself, peering up the alley. But he knew it was useless, he wasn't even going to shout after her. She'd only come back when she was ready, when and *if*.

In the sitting-room Lesley sat crying. 'I *told* you not to touch the drawer, Malcolm,' she sobbed. 'Cats are very touchy, when they've just given birth. She may never come back, you know. They're like that.'

'Well, I'm touchy too,' Slob grunted, going back to his chicken legs. 'What about my new clothes? Cost me a bomb, they did. It's disgusting.' But you could see he felt uneasy. Lesley wasn't the weeping type.

'What have you done with the kittens?' Frank whispered.

'Nothing yet,' Malc snarled at him, 'but I feel like bloody drowning them. I'd have done it already upstairs but the bath's got a load of bleach in it. It stinks too, nearly as much as those cats.'

'They *don't* stink, Malcolm, and if you dare lay a finger on them, I'll never speak to you again. Here, you can have this back, I'll speak to you when you've calmed down, and not before. I'm going home.'

Lesley wiggled the cheap blue ring off her finger and dumped it under Malcolm's nose, on the Kentucky Fried box. The room had suddenly gone very quiet and Slob just sat there staring at the ring, grease dribbling down from one corner of his mouth. Fat girls like Lesley Rathbone had a hard time looking dignified but at that moment she managed it. 'Well, I'll see you around, Malcolm,' she said quietly, and she went off through the back door.

'What about the cats, though?' Frank said, going after her, but he stayed on the step, so that Slob could see them talking. He reckoned he was safe as long as he had cover from Lesley. Otherwise he might have got a karate chop between the shoulder blades.

'I wouldn't touch them. Leave this door open and let's hope she comes back. If she's not home by tomorrow morning, phone me.'

'But what do we do if she doesn't show up? Will they die?'

'Dunno. Let's cross that bridge when we come to it. See you, Frank.'

'See you.'

He watched her walk across to the gate, tottering slightly on her high heels, then looked vaguely round again for Flump 1. She'd always been terrified of Malcolm and the row in the bedroom had obviously been too much for her.

Before going inside Frank stood in the middle of the backyard and shut his eyes tight. Feeling a bit of a fraud he said firmly, 'Please don't let the kittens die and please let their mother come back soon.'

The strength of his own feelings overwhelmed him. He cared desperately that all would be well with those two helpless, squirming scraps of fur. Was this 'Love'? Was he somehow sharing in what parents felt, in what Dad felt? And was this, in some way, a little taste of that great big love that Maggie and the nuns stood for?

Silently he repeated his prayer a second time. He'd never been able to imagine that there was anyone up there listening, but anything was worth a try. The nuns were always at it and Maggie had told him that you could pray about anything. Anyhow, he felt desperate.

The gas-fire was still hissing quietly but the sitting-room was empty now. Slob's plate contained two gnawed chicken legs and three cold chips. With a nasty cold feeling Frank went through the hall, mounted the stairs and went into the bathroom. He peered down into the water, expecting to see two dead furry lumps, but Dad's shirt was still there, slightly brownish now from the bleach. Frank swirled it around a bit, then went across the landing into the front bedroom.

Slob was lying on his bed, smoking furiously and staring at the ceiling. He edged past, half expecting a fist to come lashing out at him, or a kick from the big black

131

boots. But Malcolm didn't budge. He looked very upset, almost ready to cry.

The drawer containing the kittens was right in the middle of the room. It looked as if Slob had pulled it out in a rage and as if Lesley had wrenched it off him. Somehow, in the fight, it had landed the right way up, half-way between the bed and the Put-U-Up.

Frank stared down at it. The two blind kittens were squirming about helplessly on top of the designer clothes. At least they were still alive but their feeble, bird-like cheeping went right through him. They were hungry and bewildered and they wanted their next feed. If only the mother would come back.

'I don't know what to do, Malcolm,' he said in a small voice.

'Use a fountain-pen filler. Feed them with that. It's what they do in books.'

'Haven't got one. Anyhow, I wouldn't know how to do it. I wish you'd not touched them; we could have transferred them to that box in a day or so.'

Malc didn't reply, but at least he'd left the drawer where it was. That was because of Lesley. She wasn't the sort that made idle threats, and he was obviously dead keen on her.

Frank put his hands round the drawer to pick it up.

'*Leave it!*' Slob yelled, stubbing his cigarette out and jumping up off the bed.

'But it can't stay in the middle of the floor. It'll get kicked.'

'No, it won't. Lesley said not to touch it, and we're not going to. *See?*'

'You're changing your tune, aren't you? A minute ago you said you were going to drown them,' Frank muttered daringly.

'Listen, you . . .' Slob got down on the carpet, thrust his big sweaty face adorned with its ferocious red cockscomb right under Frank's nose and grabbed hold of his ear. 'If you think I like these bleedin' things, you can

132

think again. Get it? But just for now they're staying right where they are. Get it? If you want to do something useful, why don't you go out and buy some proper cat litter. That newspaper stinks. And what do cats eat?'

'Tinned stuff,' Frank told him, hardly able to believe his ears. 'Ours aren't fussy.'

'Anything else?'

'She's been eating cheese and onion crisps lately.'

'Well, get some of them then. Here . . .' and he gave Frank a five-pound note.

'Why don't you go?'

'Because I'm not, that's why. Lesley might phone and I want to be in.'

When he came back with the stuff, Malcolm was downstairs watching Saturday sport on telly. He'd wedged the back door open a few inches with a folded newspaper and put a saucer of milk just inside. 'They're not dead yet,' he said, as Frank unloaded everything on to the table. 'They've just gone to sleep.' He definitely sounded worried though.

Frank went towards the hall door but Malcolm grabbed him. 'Leave them alone, they don't want you looking at them.' So he sat down meekly.

'Anyone phoned?' He meant Lesley of course. The birth of the two kittens on those green designer clothes was having a most peculiar effect on Malcolm; he seemed to be in the middle of some kind of brainstorm now. There he sat, slumped in front of the TV screen, with all the doors open, ears cocked for Lesley to ring and say she'd not chucked him, eyes skinned for the cat to come sliding home and snatch her kittens back from the brink of death. Malcolm was definitely in 'love' with Lesley. He'd put the blue ring on his left-hand little finger and he kept twiddling it round moodily.

'A woman phoned, for you,' he said, 'that Mrs Manning-Sanders from up Denning.'

'What did she want?'

'Didn't say.'

133

'Any message?'

'Only could you call in, if you were round that way, something to do with a scheme she'd organized. She said you knew about it.'

'Nothing else?'

'No.'

'Well, I think I'll go up there.'

'You could phone back.'

'Yes, I know, but – well, I might as well go and see what she wants.'

The truth was that he needed to talk to Maggie, about Dad mainly. He was worried about him, and about what he might do if Rita gave him the push. Anyhow, Frank wanted to get out of the house for a bit. He didn't fancy watching sport on telly all afternoon and Slob was smoking furiously. There was a real fug in the sitting-room.

'Well, don't be very long. I might go and see Arthur later, and I can't leave the back door open.' Arthur Dunkerly was a mate of Malcolm's. He worked for a TV rental firm and he had his own flat in the town centre. Slob only went to Arthur's when he was between girl-friends.

'I won't. I'll just see what's happening, then come home.'

'Frank,' Malcolm said suddenly, watching him zip up his anorak.

'What?'

'D'you think that damned cat'll ever come back?'

'Dunno, do I?'

'What are we going to do if she doesn't?' He really meant, What's going to happen about me and Lesley?

'Let's wait and see.' Frank suddenly felt years older. He seemed to be propping everybody up, now. Dad had always leaned on him for advice and now Slob was crumbling too.

'I'll only be about half an hour,' he said, stepping over the saucer of milk as he went into the yard. Then he called over his shoulder, 'Listen, why don't you switch the telly down? She might be more inclined to settle in again, if it's quiet when she comes back.' Almost before he'd finished his sentence, the roar of the football crowd had been dimmed to a muffled drone. It was amazing, this change of heart in Malcolm, and all for the love of Lesley.

'Hope she phones, Malc,' he called back, as he opened the shed to get his bike out, and in that moment he felt strangely close to him. It must be because he cared so much about Lesley that he was putting himself out for Flump 1 and her new-born kittens, and after the mess in the drawer had disgusted him so much he'd threatened to drown them.

'Love' was a curious and powerful thing, he reflected as he pedalled off towards Denning – not that he'd had much experience, with the only two females he fancied spoken for, in their various ways.

Chapter Eleven

It looked as if an unofficial residents' meeting was going on in Palace Road. When Frank drew level with the lamp-post he found Moira, Maggie and Dr Piggott standing in a huddle by the skip, outside the gate of 105.

'High time it was removed,' he heard. 'It's going to encourage rats.' But Maggie was explaining that they'd got a lot of rubbish to clear out of their cellars and that it would be sensible to do that first. She sounded perfectly reasonable and she addressed the Bust with her usual cheery smile. Yet Frank detected a firmness underneath, a streak of iron determination which, if Dr Piggott met up with, she would find unyielding. He approved. Religious people could be a bit feeble and pathetic sometimes. They let others walk all over them, like poor Miss Halliwell. But there was nothing at all feeble about Sister Maggie. She was right to stick up for the skip.

'Did you want anything special?' he said to Moira, getting off his bike. 'My brother told me you phoned.'

'Well, I just wondered if you'd given out those lists yet, and if any of your friends were interested in helping us.'

'Oh. Was that all?' Frank felt slightly cheated. He'd expected a bit of hard news from Moira, perhaps even another sighting of Foxy's motor bike.

'What do you mean, "is that all"? We're very serious about these break-ins, Frank. The people round here are

136

getting rather tired of nasty little men helping themselves to things they've bought out of hard-earned cash. It's making our lives a misery.'

He took a step back, narrowly missing Dr Piggott's bust. The hostility in Mrs Manning-Sanders's voice had unnerved him and he didn't want to mess things up at this stage, not when there was a chance of earning fifty quid out of her spy scheme.

'No,' he said in confusion, 'I just meant, well, it's just that I've not had time to speak to anyone yet like.'

'Humph,' she muttered. 'I'd have thought youngsters of your age would have leapt at a chance like that. Now I've got my teeth into this, I want to see some action,' and she gave him one of her hard stares.

'Is Tim in?' he said. He wasn't quite ready to go back home yet. The longer he stayed out, the more chance there would be of Flump 1 creeping back home, and he wanted that badly.

'No, sorry. Their father's taken them up to the cottage. I needed a quiet weekend to myself. I'm writing a paper.'

Pity. Frank wanted another look in that basement room. In spite of the mould and the frogs, his plans for their cellar were steadily expanding. In his mind's eye he could now see himself installing a quadraphonic hi-fi system, smoke detectors and concealed lighting.

'He asked me to give you this,' she said. 'His father and I are organizing it, but Cass and Tim are allowed to invite two friends each, and you were one of Tim's choices. It's on Saturday week, in our garden.'

'Thanks very much,' Frank said, taking the bright green ticket she'd produced from her pocket. It read 'Palace Road Area Residents' Association, Barbecue with Wine and Folk Music. Proceeds in aid of the Association. All tickets £5.'

His face must have fallen because Moira said hurriedly, 'Oh, yours is complimentary, Frank, you don't have to pay. But if you could rustle up a bit of interest in our neighbourhood watch scheme among your friends, get them to keep their eyes open, et cet., I'd be eternally grateful.'

He understood then. Nothing was for free in this life. Well, he'd think about it. He didn't get asked to parties much and this one might be a bit of a laugh. Perhaps Cass and some of her friends would provide the folk music. That'd be good.

'I'll go back then,' he said. He'd been hoping Maggie might somehow get him away from the other two, so he could talk to her on his own, about Dad. But she was obviously still in the throes of turning out their cellar. She'd got dirty old gloves on, and a dirty old overall, and a big black smudge on her nose.

'Any sign of those kittens yet, Frank?' she called out, as he climbed on to his bike. 'We've got mice in the kitchen,' she explained to Moira and the Bust, 'and Frank's providing us with a cat.'

'Er, not so far,' he shouted back, pedalling off. He wasn't going to spill the beans about what had happened in Bailey Street, Slob's new clothes, the drawer, the whole crazy picture. Maggie would understand but the other two definitely wouldn't. He wasn't revealing the intimate details of his family life to them. More lies. It was hopeless sometimes, the way you got trapped.

'*Mice?*' Dr Piggott was saying, the bust rising visibly. 'Now look here, Sister Martha . . .'

'Mary actually, Mary Magdalen.'

'Well, Mary then. Now listen, it's rubbish like this which encourages rodents and if you –'

'See you then,' Frank shouted, to nobody in particular, as he went off down the road. If they were going to have a row about the skip, they could have it without him.

'Frank!' Maggie yelled after him, chopping off the fuming Dr Piggott in mid-sentence. 'We've fixed Blackpool for Easter Tuesday, OK?'

'Great.'

A barbecue with folk music on Easter Saturday and

the Blackpool trip three days later. His social life was hotting up. It was only when he thought about it in detail that he decided the Manning-Sanders affair might be a bit peculiar. If Moira was organizing the cooking, how would she cope with steaks and stuff? That's what people normally had at outdoor parties, but she was a vegetarian. What must meatless meatballs be like? And hamless hamburgers? He'd probably go to it, just to find out.

When he got home Malc was in the sitting-room with the telly switched off, all spruced up and rattling his car keys.

'Did the cat come back then?'

'Nope.'

'Did Lesley phone?'

'Nope, and I'm going to see Arthur. I might stay overnight. I'm not sitting round all day waiting for her. I'm fed up.'

Frank stole a glance at him as he sat in the chair, irritably swishing the keys round on his index finger. His mood had undergone a subtle change since dinner time; he was hardening up again.

'What about Dad?' Frank asked tentatively. 'You know what he's like.' Mr Tanner worried sick if Malcolm disappeared for the night without reporting home. He'd got an over-developed imagination.

'Oh, I've told him; he rang while you were out.'

'How did he sound?'

Slob shrugged. 'Well, it's definitely off with Rita, and a good thing too if you ask me. They're all the same, women.'

Frank was silent. He wanted to say that he hoped Malcolm wasn't bracketing Lesley together with Rita Stone. Lesley was OK. Till this morning she'd always stuck up for Slob, even when he was making everybody's life a misery with his silly rages. But saying something to that effect would be too great a risk. The vanishing cat had brought the two brothers together briefly but that unexpected, softer side of Malcolm had already been firmly covered up again. If he said anything, Frank might get thumped for 'interfering'.

'What am I going to do then?' he said grumpily, 'if you go to Arthur's?' The whole of the evening stretched boringly before him, Saturday night when boy met girl, and went out on the town.

'I don't know, do I? Someone ought to be here, in case that cat shows up. Anyhow, Dad'll be back about ten. That's what he said, anyhow.'

'What if Lesley phones, Malcolm?' Frank called down the hall as his brother opened the front door.

'Tell her I'm not available. Two can play at her game.'

Gloomily, with a mini gale blowing in from the yard through the open door, Frank went into the kitchen and made himself beans on toast. There was a small leg of lamb in the fridge, which was something. It meant that Dad was going to attempt one of his Sunday roast dinners tomorrow. There was also a big apple pie on the shelf below. He prodded at the pastry crust suspiciously. It was rock hard. This was obviously a Madge creation, though he'd not taken delivery of it himself. Perhaps she and Dad had met at last, on the doorstep? If Slob had met her, there'd have been a few sarcastic comments by now about an interfering traffic warden trying to blackmail him into silence with a bit of home cooking. Dad himself hadn't mentioned meeting Madge, though he'd chewed his way through some of her oatmeal cookies the other night. Up till now he'd been too busy concentrating on his romance with Rita.

After his beans and two cups of tea Frank settled down to watch telly, but after a few minutes he had to abandon it. The set was doing its blizzards-in-the-highlands act again, covering everything on screen with dazzling white spots. It was a very old model with what Dad called an 'intermittent fault', something he usually cured by fiddling with the aerial socket at the back. Frank

140

wasn't going to try that in case he got electrocuted. Instead, he tried the Slob treatment, thumping the top a couple of times, and swearing. When that didn't work he switched off in disgust. There wasn't much on anyhow. He could have gone up and watched Malc's portable but it was cold in the bedroom.

So he cleared the sitting-room table and got his 'Our Town' project out. It was due in on Monday and he'd still got a load of copying up to do. If he got on with it now he'd be finished by tomorrow afternoon, then he might go up and see Maggie. But in spite of the draught round his ankles from the back door, he started to feel drowsy after an hour on his project. Everything he'd scribbled down in pencil had to be rubbed out and inked in very neatly, and he seemed to be looking up every other word in the dictionary, because he couldn't spell. He wasn't at all convinced he was going to win the hundred pounds. Miss Halliwell had said it was OK to do it in your own writing, but he felt depressed when he thought about Tim's electric typewriter and that word processor Amy Chauncey was using. Anyhow, who was really interested in what dud papers like the *Spotlight* and the *Examiner* revealed about life in Darnley-in-Makerfield? His project seemed to consist of golden wedding photographs, robbers stealing electric hair-rollers, and endless Sunday School Anniversary Queens, each one more spotty and toothier than the last. Who cared about any of that? It was boring, and he was boring, and he hadn't got the remotest chance of winning.

In a fit of disgust he collected all his papers together and shoved them back on top of the dresser. Then he wrote a note to Dad, explaining about Flump 1 and why the door was open, and went upstairs. He'd get into bed and watch Slob's portable TV for a bit. It was the best way of making himself sleepy and he couldn't think of anything better to do tonight.

When he looked at the kittens he got worried. They'd not actually died; he could see their minute chests

141

fluttering rapidly in and out. But they did seem terribly still, and weak. When he put out a little finger and touched one it moved towards his hand, rooting about blindly to be fed. Frank felt like crying, 'No go, mate,' he whispered softly. 'But she'll be back soon, then you can have your supper.' But his bones told him it was hopeless. He ought to try the fountain-pen treatment perhaps, otherwise he might be burying them in the morning.

His father came back just as *Cagney and Lacey* was finishing. It had been the one programme worth watching all night, but he'd still dropped off to sleep before the end. Dad woke him by switching the telly off and trying to pull the clothes up without disturbing him.

'You OK?' he murmured, sitting up and rubbing his eyes.

It was a silly question because his father looked terrible, not ill exactly, it was nothing physical, but as if a light inside him had been switched off. This 'light', the thing that kept you going as a human being, had been weak for months, steadily dwindling as his hopes dwindled; now it had gone out completely.

'Well, son,' his father replied in a dead-pan voice. 'I'm as OK as I'll ever be and that's all I'm saying at the moment.'

'What happened with Rita then?' Frank knew already but he wanted to hear it for himself, just in case Slob hadn't told him the full story.

Mr Tanner smiled weakly and gave a peculiar little laugh, but there was no warmth in his face. It was like seeing a skeleton crack a joke.

'Oh, Rita . . . well, in a nutshell, we were talking things over in her flat when her husband walked in. She'd not really told me the truth, you see. As I understood it, it was all over months ago, they were legally separated, the lot, and she was free to marry. It turned out he'd been away on a long business trip, that's all. She knew he was coming back, but not when. Pathetic,

142

isn't it? I'm pathetic. She more or less told me that herself.'

'That's what comes of trusting people, Frank,' he added. 'I won't be trusting anyone again though, I've learned my lesson.'

'I'm sorry, Dad.' But Frank knew his father would 'trust' again. It was in his nature to love and trust people. When you got the wrong person though, love like that caused pain.

'Why didn't you tell her where to get off?' he asked. 'At least you could have –'

'Leave it, Frank. I know you're trying to help but leave it. Go to sleep, it's quite late.'

So he snuggled down obediently in the bed. 'Goodnight then, Dad,' he whispered through the blankets.

'Good-night, son. I've just left the kitchen window open, for that cat. We can't go to bed with the door unlocked. It'll be back by morning.'

'Hope so,' Frank said, though he wasn't banking on it. He was more realistic about life than Dad was.

'One thing about Malcolm staying with Arthur, son, you do get a bed to sleep in. We'll really have to do something about this room. It's a disgrace.'

'That'd be good,' and Frank closed his eyes again.

In the middle of the night something woke him up. He felt underneath his pillow for his bicycle lamp and flashed it nervously round the room. What if somebody had squeezed in through that kitchen window?

But he couldn't see anything unusual, no suspicious legs disappearing round the door, nobody hiding under the Put-U-Up with Slob's radio and Walkman under his jacket. Yet he'd definitely heard something. It had sounded like the front door.

He got out of bed and shone the bike lamp round more slowly. This time he did spot something unexpected but it wasn't one of Moira's 'miserable pilferers'; it was Flump 1, sitting in her drawer as right as ninepence.

Underneath, the kittens were guzzling away for dear life.

'You little fraud,' Frank whispered in delight, kneeling down for a closer look. 'What have you been up to then? Me and Malcolm were dead worried about you.' The cat blinked at him then started to wash herself vigorously. She was brilliant, the way she could do two things at once.

He switched the bike lamp off again, in case it unsettled her, then crept out on to the landing. Dad's door was ajar as usual, and the light turned right down on the dimmer switch, but when he peeped into the back bedroom he could see that the bed was empty and hadn't been slept in.

'Dad?' he called down the stairs, then '*Dad!*' It was half past one in the morning and he'd never been all on his own at night before. He felt panicky. He'd definitely heard noises down below. Someone had woken him up by shutting that door. Going forward a couple of steps he stopped, and listened again.

Silence. Then he heard very faint bumping noises, then another door opening and shutting. It was the cellar this time because that door always scraped when you pulled it. '*Dad!*' He was shouting very loudly now. Who was in their cellar in the middle of the night? And why wasn't his father tucked up in bed in his normal fashion, all huddled down in his blankets like a balding sausage roll?

'What?' His father sounded furious. 'And what are you doing out of bed?'

'It's – I – well, I heard something. It woke me up.'

'Look, it's only me. I can't sleep so I'm just sorting a few things out.'

'In the cellar?'

'Listen, just get back to bed, will you, and shut your door if you don't want to be disturbed.'

Puzzled, Frank did as he was told, except that he left the door open a few inches. His father sounded really

144

angry and he was suspicious, nervous too, in case he was planning to do something stupid like walk out on them. That's what some parents did when they couldn't 'cope' any more. It had happened to Marlene Braith-waite in their class, except that it was her mum that went.

He lay awake in the dark for ages, wondering what his father was up to and trying to identify the muffled thumps and bumps that drifted up intermittently from below. But he must have dozed off eventually because when he came round it was nearly light outside, and time to get up for his Sunday paper round.

Flump 1, exhausted by yesterday's adventures, was flat out in the drawer with the kittens crawling hopefully over her. In the back room Dad slept too, but on top of the bed, and still in his clothes, Frank noticed.

He went off to Wendy News without making his usual early-morning cup of tea, but he did spend a few minutes in the cellar. What on earth had his father been up to last night?

At first he thought nothing was different, except that the mould on the chimney-breast was now like a brilliant gold-green carpet. Funny how applying the new paint had actually seemed to have brought it on; there'd not been much mould before.

He inspected Dad's assortment of paint tins and decided some were missing, all those cans of bright green Buckingham gloss he'd bought the other week. He hadn't been down in the cellar for a while – he was nervous about the frogs – and anyhow, he didn't like looking at the Tesco-wrapped madonna which he ought to have given back. So he didn't know just when his father had removed the green paint. Not last night though, surely? Nobody did home-decorating jobs at half-past one in the morning. Though his father had been behaving very oddly lately, going off at funny times and not saying where.

He'd got his foot on the bottom step, ready to go up

again, when he noticed something sticking out of the cubby hole under the stairs. It was a piece of polythene sheeting, obviously covering something up.

He went over and pulled, and the plastic slid off, revealing an eighteen-inch television set. It was quite new, a Hitachi, a bigger version of the one Slob had bought for their bedroom.

His heart was racing so much as he pedalled across Larkfield towards Wendy News that he thought he was having palpitations. Before he'd found that telly he'd thought that Dad perhaps needed to do his decorating jobs outside the normal hours, to avoid the tax man. For proof he'd been going to look out for a bright green fence or a bright green garage as he rode to South Parade, something that hadn't been green before this morning.

But that TV set stuffed under the stairs in its polythene shroud offered a much more likely and more ghastly explanation of his father's nocturnal toings and froings. He must be on the same game as Foxy, and Moira's 'miserable pilferers', doing the odd bit of thieving himself, to keep the wolf from the door of Number 14 Bailey Street.

Chapter Twelve

When he got back from his round the house was still quiet and there were no signs that Dad had been downstairs. He was famished after pedalling round Denning for an hour and a half in the drizzle, and his arms ached. Sunday newspapers weighed a ton.

He switched the gas-fire up to maximum because the sitting-room felt chilly, then pottered about, filling up the kettle for a hot drink and making himself a big pile of toast. At least it was going to be a peaceful sort of day. With luck, Malcolm wouldn't be back until the evening and there was that leg of lamb in the fridge. Over a quiet Sunday dinner, perhaps he could persuade his father to tell him what was going on.

When the pot of tea he'd made had brewed for three minutes, he poured a cup out and went upstairs with it. 'Dad,' he said softly, pushing the door open. 'It's nearly half-past eight. I've brought you a drink.'

There was a little moany noise from the bed and the old-fashioned pink eiderdown billowed up and settled again as the body underneath shifted position. '*Dad*,' Frank repeated, 'do you want this or not? And should I switch the oven on yet, for the joint?'

Slowly, like the school tortoise emerging from its winter sleep, Mr Tanner's bald round head poked out reluctantly from under the covers. A pale washed-out face peered round blearily for a minute than dropped

147

back on the pillow, accompanied by another moan. A red plastic bucket had been strategically positioned by the bedside table, and the room smelt of sick.

'Aren't you well then?' Frank shifted the *Flatten That Stomach!* book and the empty Overnight Success packets to one side, and set down his cup and saucer. Mr Tanner gave a groan and turned over. 'Dad, *say* something, for heaven's sake . . .'

Through the rosy eiderdown the reply was muffled. 'I feel terrible. I've been up half the night, in the bathroom. It's obviously a bug I've got; I'm staying here for a bit.'

'So don't you want this tea then?' Frank's voice was reasonably sympathetic but underneath he was sceptical. He and Dad were alike. If something worried them it went straight to their insides. When they had school exams, for example, Frank always had to go to the cloakroom just before, and the night he'd taken Maggie's madonna he'd been in and out of the bog for hours.

He picked up the cup of tea and went to the door. Then he looked back. 'Dad,' he said, 'what's that new telly doing in the cellar?'

Silence, then a muffled grunt.

'You what?'

He heard what sounded like 'Mind your own business, can't you?', but his father hadn't risked shoving his head out and it was a shrewd move. His face would have told Frank straight away if he'd pinched it, you could read him like a book.

But he decided to have one last go. 'What did you say, Dad?'

'I said, *"Mind your own business!"* ' This time he'd emerged for a split second, red-faced and wild-looking, only to burrow back into his steamy nest again.

'Pardon me for breathing,' Frank muttered, pulling the door shut. Then he went into the bathroom and emptied the rejected tea down the plug-hole.

By mid-morning the drizzle of the early hours had turned into a thick downpour. There was no way he could go out, even if he'd got somewhere to go, and chance would be a fine thing. For want of something better to do he got his project out again, sorted through all the papers and carried on with the copying up. He wasn't going to win the hundred pounds, but Miss Halliwell had mentioned 'runners-up' prizes. Even ten quid would be better than nothing.

The gas-fire hissed, the lamb spat and bubbled in the oven and his hand moved monotonously across the pages, covering them with big loopy handwriting. Then something rubbed up against his legs, mewing to be let out. Flump 1 had come down from the bedroom.

'Good cat,' Frank told her, tickling her ears. She must feel properly re-established to have left the kittens on their own. 'Sorry the old man's not been round to see his offspring,' he added. Though, in a way, it was quite useful that Flump 2 had taken to staying out for days on end. Lesley had told him he could have attacked the babies out of jealousy and Frank felt they'd got enough to cope with, just being born. He was thinking about Lesley, and copying out another toaster robbery, when the phone rang and it was her. She wanted to know if Flump 1 had come back, and also where Slob was.

When he'd explained and rung off, he wasn't quite sure he'd done the right thing, giving her Arthur Dunkerley's number. In spite of her throwing the ring back and walking out yesterday, she was obviously planning to patch things up now. By rights Malcolm ought to come crawling to her with gratitude, but you could never tell with him. He might get into one of his awkward moods and give her the cold shoulder. It had happened once before after a tiff. *Love* . . . Frank didn't begin to understand it.

Anyhow, she'd been thrilled about Flump 1 coming back and she said he could move the drawer into a corner now, to stop them tripping over it. In a day or so she thought the cat would probably transfer the kittens to the baked-beans carton herself. So why didn't Frank move it up into the bedroom now, just in case?

He was half-way up the stairs with the box when the phone rang again. This time it was Gran Corcoran, in one of her 'hurt' moods. She wanted to know why Dad hadn't been round for his usual Sunday morning coffee.

When Frank explained about the stomach upset, she said she'd come straight down with something for their dinners. But with a little skilful embroidery of the truth he managed to put her off. First, he said the bug was bound to be infectious; second, that Dad was too ill to get out of bed; third, that their gas-fire had broken and it was only fifty degrees in the sitting-room. He knew that'd do it because she lived in a permanent seventy-degree fug and never took her thermals off, even in summer.

The truth was that Frank felt he couldn't stick a whole day of Gran. She'd be bound to go on about that funny church she went to, and about getting 'in touch' with the dead. Sometimes she even talked about 'contacting' his mother and he really hated that.

He met Dad on the landing, returning from another visit to the bathroom, on wobbly legs. He'd got his pyjamas on now so he'd obviously got no plans to get up and face reality in the near future. 'Who phoned?' he said, quite sharply. 'Anyone for me?'

Frank stared at him. Who was he expecting? And what had he done in the wee small hours, to put that guilty, worried-rabbit expression on his face?

'Only Gran. She wanted to come over but I said you weren't up to it. I've got the lamb on so we won't starve,' and he grinned at him. But Mr Tanner wasn't in a grinning mood. 'Who else?' he said. 'It rang twice.'

'Lesley. She wanted to know about the cats, and

where our Malcolm was. I told her he'd gone to
Arthur's.'

'Oh.' Dad looked distinctly relieved. 'That's all right
then. Well, I'm going back to bed for a bit. Nobody's
knocked on the door, have they?'

'No.'

'Well, if they do, I'm in bed. Get it?'

'OK.'

'And I don't want to be disturbed. OK?'

'*OK*. Listen, Dad, what's up?'

But his father had already gone into the back bedroom
and closed the door.

It was quarter to one and he'd turned the joint up for the
last quarter of an hour. Madge had phoned, to ask if
the kittens had arrived, and he'd consulted her about
cooking a roast. He was doing mashed potatoes and peas
with the lamb and they were having her apple pie for
afters. It might be semi-edible with custard sloshed all
over it and that looked easy enough to make.

There hadn't been any lavatory noises for the last hour
or so, so it must mean Dad's insides were settling down
again. Frank hoped he'd be up to eating some of this
dinner; he was feeling quite proud of it.

He was just setting the table, glasses, paper napkins,
vegetable dishes, all very neat, when the letter-box rattled. He went through into the hall and stared at the
front door. Through the frosted-glass panel at the top he
could see what looked like a very large head and behind
it, out on the street, a blue light was flashing. That meant
only one thing.

His stomach did a triple somersault and he froze in
the doorway, then he twisted round to see a portion of
red and white pyjama trousers being whisked out of
sight, at the top of the stairs. Then he stared at the front
door again. The blurred head was still there and the
letter-box was being rattled a second time. As he
watched, two pudgy fingers were shoved through the

151

slit and wiggled about. 'Anyone at home?' a voice called. It sounded quite friendly for a policeman. Frank had no doubt at all that it was one.

He opened the door to a short square man with a big moustache and thick glasses, not in uniform like the policeman at his side, but a detective-inspector something or other. He couldn't take in what it said on the identity card; he was beyond rational behaviour now. All his worst fears were being confirmed.

'We'd like to speak to your father, Frank. It is Frank, isn't it? And your father's Mr Feargus Tanner. Is that correct?'

'Yes, but he's not very well this morning,' Frank gobbled at him helplessly. 'He was up half the night with collywobbles. He's got a funny stomach.'

'Well, if you'd just tell him we're here and that we'd like a quick word with him. He can come down in his pyjamas. Or we'll go up. It's all the same to us.'

Frank turned and bolted, falling up the stairs in his panic. Dad was back under his eiderdown but no longer cocooned. Instead he was lying flat on his back with his arms stuck out at right angles, staring rigidly at the ceiling, like a lamb on the altar of sacrifice.

'Dad, there are two men downstairs. One's in police uniform and the other's in plain clothes. I think you'd better come.'

He wouldn't have been surprised if his father had hit him one, thrown a mad screaming fit, or jumped out of the window. Instead he got straight out of bed, gathered up yesterday's trousers from a chair, selected clean socks, shirt and underpants from various drawers and went into the bathroom.

'Tell them I'll be down in five minutes,' he said in a tight little voice. 'I need a good wash. Let them wait in the front room. You can switch the fire on.'

So Frank went down again and reported that his father was just 'freshening up'. He still didn't know what crime he'd committed but he was secretly impressed that he

152

was preparing to meet his end with dignity, and in a clean shirt.

The quick word took nearly an hour. Before he joined the two men in the front room, Dad stopped in the hall and told Frank to 'get on with something'. His voice came out all choked and strangled and his face was chalky-white now. Frank had never felt so distanced from him before, and never so lonely, as he crouched against the door with his ear pressed against it. There was no way he was carrying on with 'Our Town' or anything else when Dad was in there, undergoing the Spanish Inquisition with those two men.

Through the big brass keyhole he could see them all huddled round the gas-fire. The front room was cluttered up with a load of electrical appliances Dad had acquired through the small ads, for repair and resale. He'd not done much with them though; he'd been waiting for that vital injection of cash from the Friendly Northern.

Frank spent ages with his ear crushed against the door, but he couldn't work out much of what they were saying. He only got the odd word. 'Bank' was mentioned several times, and 'loan application', and when they discussed this bit he could hear Dad getting quite agitated, with the two men calming him down. Then it all turned into a low burble again, impossible to separate into meaningful sentences. He never heard the word 'television' though, not once, and nobody went down the cellar to inspect that Hitachi.

As he crouched on the hall lino, with stiff knees and a sore ear, he suddenly caught a strong whiff of something. The joint had been left on high, to crisp up, but it was obviously burning now. He did a silent frogleap away from the door and dived into the kitchen. The air was blue and thick and before opening the oven he flung the back door open, flapping the smoke out.

The leg of lamb wasn't exactly on fire but it was next door to it and he carried the blackened roasting tin across the kitchen, dumping it on the draining-board to cool off under the window. It was much smaller now, not so much a leg any more as an ankle, and a little one at that. Madge had warned him that meat could 'shrink', but this was ridiculous.

He was poking at it miserably with a fork, when Dad came into the kitchen with his coat on. 'I've got to go into town and answer a few questions, Frank,' he said, 'just routine, nothing to worry about. I'll explain when I get back.' But the way he said it meant '*Don't ask me what it's about*' and Frank, who'd opened his mouth to ask just that, shut it again abruptly.

'Our phone number's on this, Frank,' the beefy, plain-clothes man said genially, leaning over Dad's shoulder and giving him a little card. 'Ring if you want to speak to your dad, but we shouldn't be too long. All right?'

'All right,' Frank muttered.

Before following them down the hall, Dad put an arm round his shoulder and gave it a little squeeze. 'Explain to Malcolm, if he's back before I am,' he said.

'Explain *what*?' Frank was near to tears now.

'Well, you know.'

Seconds later he stood at the front window watching the police car going off down Bailey Street. At least the blue light wasn't flashing any more, so hopefully it meant Dad wasn't bound for prison, just 'answering a few questions' like the men had said.

When they'd gone out of sight, he went back into the kitchen and stared sadly at the ruined ankle of lamb, the neatly set table, the red paper napkins folded into fans. All that effort and nobody left to appreciate it.

Alone in the quiet of the house, with the rain still thudding against the windows, Frank pulled a chair out, sat down, and began to cry.

He saw no one at all till five o'clock, and no one phoned. Then Slob came back. Before he could say anything his brother said, 'I've heard from Dad, he rang me at Arthur's. Glad that damned cat turned up anyhow.'

'What on earth's he been doing, Malcolm? He's been gone ages and I've been stuck here on my own all day.' People felt more important than cats to him, just at the moment.

The only good thing was that he'd finished 'Our Town'. A whole afternoon of mindless copying up and checking spellings in the dictionary had been a welcome escape route. While he'd been doing that he'd deliberately not thought about his father, and about what might be happening down at the police station. 'Well, what has he been up to?' he repeated.

'Search me,' grunted Malc.

'But he's been away hours.'

'Well, there'll be some reason. Don't get your knickers in a twist about it. Remember when they interviewed him once before, when he bought that stuff off the market? It'll be that kind of thing. Anyhow, I've got something that'll interest you in the back of the car, wait on,' and he went outside again.

Frank had forgotten all about the market episode but, now Slob mentioned it, it made sense. Relief began to trickle through him as he remembered the police coming round about a year ago, after Dad had bought some old electrical stuff off a stall. It had all been nicked and the police had returned everything to the owners.

Malc might be right, this could be that again, but on a bigger scale. If it was though, why hadn't his father *explained*? And why had he been so uptight with nerves that he'd spent half the night in the bog? It didn't suggest an easy conscience.

He was still brooding about it when Slob came back from the car carrying a video recorder. 'Where's that come from?' Frank said, running a suspicious eye over it for the Manning-Sanders's secret number. He'd got thieving on the brain now.

'Arthur lent it me, didn't he? I'm going to hitch it to the upstairs telly, it's better reception.'

'Not much use if you've got no films though, is it?' Frank said miserably.

But Malcolm had used Arthur's card and been to Video Scene in town. 'Take a look at them then, Clever-clogs.'

Frank read the labels on the two boxes, *Vampires in the House of Death* and *Return of the Blob*. Malcolm had always been crazy about horror films; the more blood and guts that got spattered across the screen the better. He was obviously planning a jolly evening in front of the box. 'Want to watch one of them with me?' he said.

'Why? Isn't Lesley coming round?' It wasn't like Malcolm to include his kid brother in anything.

'Nope.'

'But she did phone you, didn't she?'

'Yep.'

'So –'

'Well, I told her I'd got something else on tonight, didn't I? I told her she could cool it for a bit, if you want to know.'

'But –'

'Look, mind your own business, you.'

Frank had got it right then, about those two. Lesley had gone just a bit too far, giving Slob his ring back. Underneath his red rooster hairdo he was obviously sensitive, like the rest of the human race, and he'd decided to play hard to get for a bit.

'I said you can watch one of these with me, if you want. Take your pick.' But Frank could smell beer on his breath. The first few drinks always cheered him up, but if he carried on drinking he usually turned nasty, and he'd brought some cans of beer in with the videos.

Frank turned the film boxes over and opted for *Return of the Blob*. They might get a few laughs out of it, but if Malcolm drank too much, or started picking his feet and

156

throwing the skin about, he'd come downstairs again and wait for Dad on his own.

The front door banged when the Blob had been going for about twenty minutes. Frank left Malcolm watching a pink jelly-like monster engulfing a whole McDonald's in California and rushed downstairs. His father was sitting by the gas-fire, still wearing his outdoor coat.

'Dad?'

No answer.

'*Dad?* Any news?' Frank sat down in the other chair and waited.

'Great news actually.' But his voice was weak and wispy like the voice of Maggie's old men, and his face had a crushed, defeated look. It wasn't the face of someone bearing 'great news' at all.

'So what's that then?'

'Remember Fred Huggett, the foreman from Morland's Electrical? Well, he's taken me on for two weeks. He's got a big job on, over in Leeds, and they need extra people. They're picking me up at half-past seven tomorrow, so you'll have to get yourself to school. OK? That's why I'm so late; I went up to see him on the off-chance, like.'

'So you've not been with the police at all. I mean, not till now?'

'Oh no, I was only with them for a bit. Then I thought I'd better drop in on your gran. Then I went to see Fred. He lives in her street, you know.'

'Well, you might have told me what you were doing, Dad. I was sat here worrying.'

'Listen, I'm sorry, son. I'd got a lot on my mind.'

'So what about the police then? What did they want?'

'Frank,' Mr Tanner said slowly, 'I really don't want to talk about it just now, it's too complicated. The chances are that we won't hear any more about it. No point in worrying yourself silly, now is there?'

'But, Dad . . .'

157

'Listen, have I ever let you down in the past?'

'No, but that's not –'

'Have I ever told you lies?'

'No.'

'Right, well just believe what I say, that it's going to be *all right*. OK?'

Frank didn't answer. He watched his father take his coat off, fill the kettle and start bustling about. He wasn't in the least satisfied with the feeble explanation he'd just heard and he felt badly let down, sitting in the house all day, imagining all sorts. Faces sometimes told you more than words and tonight Dad looked a defeated, frightened man. He hoped they'd seen the last of the police at 14 Bailey Street but he wouldn't place bets on it. One thing he was certain about was that his father wouldn't say anything else, and it was no use trying to make him.

For supper Mr Tanner scraped the burnt bits off the ankle of lamb and slapped meat between slices of bread and butter. Frank hadn't eaten anything since breakfast; nerves about Dad and the law had gone to his stomach and he'd not felt like it. But watching his father munching away brought real hunger on, and he bit into one of the thick double doorsteps himself, and chewed.

Burnt ankle of lamb sandwiches were an entirely new taste sensation.

The phone rang three times before bed-time and Dad kept leaping up to answer, as if it was in danger of exploding. All the calls were very long but Frank knew better than to ask what they were about. His father was broody and silent, and during the evening he had two little glasses of whisky, 'for his nerves'. It was a bad sign.

He'd gone off to Leeds in Fred Huggett's van by the time Frank came down next morning and they didn't see each other till nearly six o'clock. Then it was 'How was school today, son?' and 'Did you get your project in on time?', a whole string of polite little questions to deflect the all-important big one that Frank wanted to ask – just why had the police taken him down for questioning the day before?

He said school had been 'fine', but it hadn't. All day the people in their class had been giving him funny looks and talking about him in little groups. It definitely wasn't his imagination. He'd heard 'Frank Tanner' and 'Tanner's Dad' and 'Bailey Street' several times in the playground, and people were laughing about something. Tim had been odd too. Instead of hanging round him at break and during the dinner hour, he'd gone out of his way to avoid him. Cass had given her usual wave at home time, when she'd joined up with Barry Townsend at the school gates, but she'd had a distinctly embarrassed look on her face.

Everyone stared and whispered on the Tuesday as well. He couldn't see Tim at all at break, and at dinner time he saw him take his packed lunch to the other end of the canteen when they usually sat together. It was very peculiar.

Perhaps that ankle of lamb had given him a funny body odour? Or perhaps he'd suddenly developed bad breath? How could you tell though, without asking someone? And nobody seemed to want to speak to Frank Tanner any more.

It wasn't till he got home that night that he found out the reason. He was sitting in front of the telly with a bowl of cornflakes, both cats on his knee, when he heard the letter-box flap rattle.

Well, it couldn't be Dad and it couldn't be Malcolm. Dad was working late for Fred Huggett and Malcolm had softened, and gone over to Lesley's. The big romance was on again.

It wasn't anybody at all, just the mid-week *Examiner* from Midwood's, lying on the door mat. He tucked it under his arm and went back to the sitting-room. Being a newsboy and doing the 'Our Town' project had got him very interested in newspapers. If he learned to spell better, he could be a reporter when he left school.

What daft headline had the *Examiner* dreamed up tonight then? Whoever wrote them had a corny sense of humour; they could be quite entertaining sometimes. But what he read, in big black letters across the front page, didn't strike him as at all funny. In capitals two inches high it said:

LOCAL MAN PAINTS BANK GREEN.

Chapter Thirteen

Next morning he was out of the house by half past five. He'd gone to bed very early the night before, and pretended to be fast asleep when Dad came home. That way they didn't have to talk to each other. The front page of the newspaper was folded up small in his jeans pocket. Not that it would stop his father seeing the article. A placard outside Midwood's newsagent's already said 'Darnley Man in Bank Outrage', and it was bound to be in the *Spotlight* too. The story must be all over town by now.

It was still dark when he reached Shorrock Street, but there was a street lamp opposite the squat concrete and timber hut that housed Dad's branch of the Friendly Northern. He propped his bike against it and stared across the road, a sour sick feeling in his stomach, dragging unwilling eyes upward till they were level with the building opposite. *Please don't let it be true.*

But it was. Dad was very nifty with his paint brushes and rollers. All the people he'd done jobs for had commented on how neat he was, how thorough, yet how quick. Well, he must have been quick, to have painted all this overnight. It was only small but it still represented several hours work for one man, and he'd done a good job too.

Frank had crossed the road and was examining his father's handiwork with hideous fascination; no runs, no drips, no brush-marks, no bits left out. The whole of the Friendly Northern Bank, Shorrock Street Branch, Darnley-in-Makerfield, was a glossy bright Buckingham green, including its flat roof, its door handles, and all its windows. Someone had made a feeble attempt to scrape some of the paint off, to see out, but it was obviously a job for the experts. According to the report, high pressure hoses were going to be necessary to restore the place to its former glory.

You could always tell if a bank belonged to the Friendly Northern because they were all painted yellow and black, with the eagle logo on the windows and doors. This shiny green hut resembled something from Legoland.

Dad must have chosen 'Buckingham' because green made you think of Ireland, land of the Shamrock, the Emerald Isle. The report in the *Examiner* said he'd done it as 'a protest', because he wanted to speak out for all the hundreds of people like him who'd gone to their banks in good faith and been turned away. '*An official at the Friendly Northern*', it had stated, '*denied that Mr Feargus Tanner's application had been turned down because he had an Irish name. "Frankly, we are bewildered," local mana-ger, Mr Brian Brocklehurst (37) said last night. "He even painted my car tyres with green paint and I am having consid-erable difficulty getting it off. He should have made his com-plaint to us in person, instead of resorting to these childish tactics." Mr Tanner, aged 45 and a widower, lives at 14 Bailey Street, Darnley with his two sons. A former electrician with Morland's Electrical, he has been unemployed for some time and said he had also recently suffered a disappointment in his private life. "I'm afraid everything just got on top of me," he told our reporter on the telephone last night. "It was a very silly thing to do and I apologize to all concerned." The Friendly Northern has yet to decide what action to take against Mr Tanner.*' Frank had read the report so many times, he'd more or less got it off by heart.

As he climbed back on to his bike he stared across at

the silly-looking green hut. True, his father had behaved like a lunatic, creeping out at dead of night to slap gloss paint all over it, and he would probably end up in debt now, for years and years. He might even go to prison for committing criminal damage. Yet deep down, Frank felt he understood.

He could see exactly how things had 'got on top' of Dad: Rita Stone taking him for a ride then ditching him; the jobs he went after that never came to anything; the bills he couldn't pay – and underneath all this, the running sore of the bank loan. He must really have believed that they'd lend him the money in the end, even though they'd said his front-room conversion scheme wasn't 'practical'.

That final refusal from Brian Brocklehurst had arrived the same day Rita had chucked him, and it had all been too much. Some people would have banged their heads against the wall and screamed; some would have gone out and got drunk. Others might have found out where the bank manager lived and punched him in the face. But Dad, silently brooding about everything for weeks and weeks, till he couldn't stand the tension any more, had crept out with all his painting tackle in the middle of the night and given vent to his disgust at life in general by painting the offending bank green.

If it had been anybody else's father Frank would probably have laughed, like the people at school. But it was his own, and he wanted to cry.

On his way back to Bailey Street he stopped at Midwood's, bought a tube of Polos and took a free *Spotlight* from the pile on the counter. Their headline was even worse than the *Examiner's* – BANK MAN SAYS IT WITH PAINT.

He ran his eyes over the report underneath. It wasn't much different from the other one, except that they said the Tanners lived at 4 Bailey Street, not 14, and that Dad was an unemployed plumber.

Well, there was no way he was going to do his paper

163

round this morning. The thought of facing Lily Chadwick with that 'Bank Man' headline splashed across her *Spotlights* turned his stomach. He couldn't imagine ever going back, now. Dad's outburst had branded him for life.

And what about the Manning-Sanderses? They obviously knew about the whole thing already. Look how Cassie and Tim had been behaving. It meant Moira must know that they lived in Bailey Street, not Baillie Terrace, that Frank was a liar and that Dad had gone mad. How could he be expected to go back to school, after this? In fact, how could he face people ever again?

As he pedalled home the sun came up. Behind the dark ugly jumble of shabby streets, run-down factories and abandoned mills, the moors spread themselves out peacefully like a shimmering green cloth. He'd walked up there with Maggie, the day they'd seen Cass with Barry Townsend, and she'd talked to him about his troubles, he remembered, talked sense too. She'd not made him feel a fool like most grown-ups did.

Sister Maggie was the only person he could talk to about all this. He'd go and see her today, instead of going to school, and while he was at it he'd take that picture back. It was getting on his nerves, sitting under the cellar sink amid the frogs; it was one complication in his life that he could sort out right now. He would just have to tell Maggie he'd pinched the picture in a moment of weakness. It couldn't make things worse than they were already.

When he got to Palace Road, he waited till he judged that everybody at the Manning-Sanderses must have gone off for the day; then he shoved his bike under its usual holly bush at 105, got the Tesco's bag off the back carrier and went up the drive with the madonna. Instead of knocking at the front he went through the side gate and peered in at the kitchen window. Sister Geraldine stood at the sink, her arms up to their elbows in soapy water. Everybody did menial tasks here, Maggie had told him, nobody was considered 'too grand' for cleaning the brasses, emptying the dustbins or washing old men's feet. It was part of what they believed, part of the 'Love of God', like it said on the gate.

Frank steeled himself, ducked out of sight and tapped on the back door. He'd have to go through with this now, even if it meant confessing about the picture to the boss.

She opened the door at once, still drying her hands on a tea-towel. 'I'd like to speak to Sister Mary,' he blurted out in a rush, but taking immediate refuge in a close inspection of his own feet. Those keen blue eyes of hers always unnerved him, the way they seemed to see through everything.

'She's not available just now,' he heard, a calm unruffled voice from the other side of a solid purple bust. 'Perhaps I could help?'

'But can't I speak to her? Just for a minute? It's urgent like.' Frank's voice was wavering now, in spite of his efforts. Why couldn't she just go and fetch Maggie? Surely she could see what a state he was in?

There was a pause, then the door was pulled open. 'Come in then, Frank. Take a seat, I'll just go and see what's happening.'

He pulled a stool out and sat waiting at the kitchen table. Some meat was simmering in a pan on the old Aga cooker. Above it, where other people would have fixed a clock, a wooden Jesus hung on a wooden cross. He'd often looked at that when he'd had cups of tea in this kitchen, with Maggie and Sister Ursula of the Teeth. That cross, she'd told him once, stood for everything the nuns believed, all the love in the world. Frank didn't really understand how someone jolly like Maggie could be associated with all that gloom and suffering. All the nuns were cheerful though, humming as they went about their menial tasks in the echoey rooms and corridors of 105. Even Sister Geraldine cracked the odd joke.

Through the kitchen door he could hear them singing a hymn. Usually, he quite liked the sound but today, with all that he'd got on his mind, solemn music like that upset him. They were obviously in the middle of a singing practice for their 'chapel', a dark narrow room at the back of the house. Maggie wouldn't be allowed to come and see him.

Gloomily, he began to fold up the two newspaper reports about Dad which he'd spread out on the table for her to read. Then he felt a hand on his shoulder and he heard the door being shut behind him. It was Maggie.

'Hi, Frank,' she said, 'how are you doing?' and she sat down at the other end of the long table.

Four feet of scrubbed pine stretched between them now, acres of wood separated them, sharpening up the panic and loneliness he felt inside. There she sat, all fresh and country-looking with her face raised to his, her neat head on one side as usual, wondering why he'd come.

But how could he tell her he'd come for comfort, that he wanted her to come to his end of the table, and put her arms round him so he could cry about Dad? That he wanted her to be the sister he'd always wanted, the mother he'd never known, not a young nun whose life was already dedicated to that mysterious thing, 'the love of God'? At that moment, he needed her more than God did. Silently, he pushed his two cuttings down to her end of the table, sliding the Tesco's carrier after them. Then he sat firmly on his hands, because they were shaking so much.

All the time she was reading the articles he watched her carefully. At first he thought she was going to laugh because her mouth twitched very slightly, now and again. Then he saw her hands go up to her face. When she dropped them she looked much more serious but he detected she was having to make an almighty effort to keep her face straight.

166

At last she said, 'I'm really very sorry, Frank,' and she pushed the two cuttings back along the table.

'What am I going to *do*, Maggie?

She shrugged and gave a little smile. 'Well, what can you do? It's not your problem, is it? Have you talked to your father?'

'No. We've been avoiding each other, but knowing him, he won't want to discuss it when I do try. I knew something must be up on Sunday, when the police came round. All he said was that it'd probably blow over and that we'd not hear any more about it. But I never realized he'd done something as daft as this. I thought he'd just nicked a telly I found in the cellar. I mean, honestly, fancy painting a *bank*. He's off his chump.'

Maggie did laugh then. 'What do you mean, Frank?' she said. 'I've never heard that expression before.'

'Well, off his rocker, like, y'know, crazy.'

'But I like crazy people! Not many people would have thought of painting the bank, as a protest, now would they? I do like it, Frank. I could just see it on television, couldn't you? It's wonderful.' She was laughing so much now that for one terrible moment Frank wanted to hit her. It wasn't 'wonderful', it was dreadful, and it might land his father in debt for years and years, if not actually in prison. She must be overtired or something because of all that cleaning and scrubbing they did in this place. She just wasn't thinking straight.

He didn't hit her, but he suddenly shouted very loudly, 'Don't laugh, Maggie, please. They were all laughing at school. They'll all have gone to look at it, knowing that lot. I can't stand it. Please don't laugh like that.'

'I'm sorry Frank,' she said at once. 'Listen, I'm sure it'll just blow over, honestly. And as for these silly news-paper stories, well, you know what reporters are like. It'll be something different tomorrow. Everybody will have forgotten the whole thing by next week, you'll see.'

'But Maggie, it's my *Dad*! They've made him sound

167

such a *fool!*' And he brought his fist crashing down on the table, making everything in the kitchen rattle.

This time she did walk round to his end. He felt her hands come down on his shaking shoulders, giving them a little squeeze. 'I do understand, Frank,' she said.

'No, you don't,' he muttered. 'How would you like it, if it was your dad? Everyone poking fun at him and that?'

There was a long pause, then she said, 'Frank dear, my old dad was a bit of a problem too, you know. He wasn't, well, original like yours but – '

'So you think it's "original", do you?' he interrupted sourly, 'painting a bank in the middle of the night, just because it won't give him a loan for a silly scheme, making everyone laugh at our family?'

'My dad,' she pressed on firmly, 'was a bit of a drinker. My brother and I were always sent to fetch him home from the bar. If my mother went they usually ended up having a fight. And we were only young, Frank, much younger than you and your Malcolm.'

'But you still don't *understand*,' he said, rubbing viciously at his raw red cheeks down which, in spite of all his efforts, the tears had started falling.

'OK, Frank. You win. Nobody understands.' Abruptly, she took her hands away from his shoulders and resumed her seat at the other end of the table.

But the tone of her voice worried him now and he got to his feet. She'd always been so kind to him before, so willing to see his side of things. Now it sounded as if he'd really hurt her feelings by losing his temper and wallowing in self-pity. Perhaps she'd ask him to leave in a minute and never come back. He couldn't bear that, not at the moment when he needed someone to stick up for him.

'I'm very sorry,' he grunted, then he rushed straight on before she could say anything else. 'But why are you so sure it'll "blow over"? It says in the *Spotlight* that the bank might sue for damages.'

But Maggie shook her head. 'I'm sure they won't, Frank.'

He stared at her. How *could* she be 'sure'? Religion wasn't supposed to be about foretelling the future, you were supposed to trust in God for that. And while they were on the subject, where was God, when Dad painted the bank? Asleep? But he'd better not say that or she'd be really offended. In confusion he sank back on to his stool and put his face in his hands. 'You just can't be sure, Maggie,' he said through his fingers. 'They might send him to prison, and he's all I've got. I love my Dad.'

'Well, of course you do, and listen, there's absolutely no way he's going to prison, so you can get that thought out of your thick head. Right? At the very most he'll have to pay something towards all the paint being cleaned off and they'll probably –'

But Frank chopped her off, the light suddenly dawning. 'You've been talking to the Manning-Sanderses, haven't you?' he said accusingly. 'You *knew*, all the time. Why on earth didn't you *say*?' He felt absolutely stupid now and, somehow, childish.

'Well, I hadn't actually seen those papers, and you wanted me to read the reports, didn't you? Anyhow, I wasn't expecting you to come round here this morning; I wasn't quite prepared. Now be reasonable, for goodness sake. It's all much less serious than it might be, that's the point.'

But it still felt very serious to him. She could shut herself away in this nunnery, say a few prayers, sing a few hymns. He had to face the outside world again.

He picked up the two cuttings and folded them up very small, as if, making them as tiny as possible, somehow diminished what Dad had done. 'BANK MAN SAYS IT WITH PAINT.' Newspaper people were vulgar and unfeeling. Whoever had dreamed that one up could have had no notion of his father's problems, the worries and the loneliness, the fears about not making ends meet. That would have been the best line to take on his 'Our Town' project, not Golden Oldies and Sunday School Queens. If only he'd thought of it before.

'So what did the Manning-Sanderses say then?'

'I've only spoken to Mrs. Mr's still in Paris, at his banking conference.'

'OK. What did she say then? She doesn't like associations with people like us you know. She's a snob, I think.'

For the first time Maggie looked genuinely angry. 'You might be sorry you said that, Frank,' she said sharply. 'She's quite concerned about you, if you must know.'

'Oh, yes,' he muttered sarcastically. 'Well, I don't want people like her looking down on me.'

She got up from her stool, came round to his side of the table, and gave him a shake. 'Frank Tanner, you should be ashamed of yourself. She rang her husband in Paris the minute she heard about your father, and she got him to make some inquiries, before things got out of hand. It's not their fault it's all over the newspapers, you know. Your dad obviously spoke to reporters and you should never do that.'

'Yes, well,' Frank said helplessly. His head was aching now and he didn't know what to think. Those long phone calls on Sunday night must have been local reporters, putting the pressure on. His father, all of a jitter after the police visit, wouldn't have known how to cope with that. He wasn't smooth, in calm control of his life like the Manning-Sanderses. All the same, Tim's mother was clearly on their side, and putting up a fight for them.

Their conversation had somehow ground to a halt and she was staring at him rather coldly, obviously waiting for him to leave. 'I'll go then,' he said, standing up suddenly and accidentally kicking his stool over in the process. He'd better disappear before things broke down altogether, so that he wouldn't be able to come back. Life wouldn't be the same if he hadn't got the nuns at 105. Perhaps Maggie needed to calm down a bit too.

'Where's Eric by the way?' he said, trying to sound casual as he went to the kitchen door. 'Are we still taking him to Blackpool?' By this time in the morning the old men had usually started knocking on the front door. They chucked them out of the hostel in town quite early.

'I hope so,' Maggie said, 'but he's not very well at the moment. They've taken him into hospital actually.'

Frank's first reaction was one of resentment. He knew it was selfish but he didn't want the old man to die just yet. He'd been hoping to take Maggie on the Big Dipper. Eric's eightieth birthday was just an excuse for a day out with her.

'I'll let you know,' she added, holding the door open.

'OK. See you.'

'See you, Frank. By the way, aren't you a bit late for school?'

'Yes, but I'm not bothered,' he called back. He wasn't going to explain that he'd decided to stay at home for the day, to avoid people. Anyhow, she'd know what a rotten coward he was about things in general, as soon as she opened that Tesco's bag he'd left on the kitchen table.

But half-way down the drive he heard her running after him. 'You've forgotten your shopping,' she told him, dumping the Tesco's carrier bag in his arms.

'But I –'

'Sorry, but I can't talk now, I ought to be in chapel. Take care crossing that dual carriageway. See you.' And he stood there helplessly, watching the front door being firmly shut.

He was never going to get that picture back to its rightful owners and in a way it wasn't his fault, he reflected rather bitterly, pedalling home.

He spent the morning watching another couple of horror films Malc had got from Video Scene. They wouldn't have scared anyone, not even in the middle of the night, and in broad daylight the 'special effects' were particularly pathetic. You could tell that the monsters were only rubber models and the blood was fake-looking, like thin orange paint. After the first few gallons had jetted out of someone's headless trunk, while the rubber monsters gambolled about cheerily over a field of corpses, Frank more or less ceased to react and goggled mindlessly, feeding Flump 1 with cheese and onion crisps. She was less manic about staying with the kittens now and spent quite long periods curled up on his knees.

The phone rang several times while he was viewing, but he didn't answer it once. It might be school, to see where he was, or Maggie, asking about the picture, or it could be another reporter after Dad. Whoever was ringing the phone was best ignored. That way he couldn't get into any more trouble.

He'd just come down from watching Malc's telly to make himself fried egg on fried bread for dinner when somebody knocked on the front door. Through the frosted glass he could see another head but this time there was no blue light flashing. Whoever it was knocked harder and the letter-box rattled. He'd better answer. He couldn't stay here all day, pretending to be dead. Anyhow, it might be vital news, a big pools win or Dad fleeing the country.

When he opened the door he found Moira Manning-Sanders on the doorstep. 'Hello Frank,' she said, coming into the hall without actually being asked, 'why aren't you at school?'

'Oh, I didn't go today,' he said flatly, as she followed him through to the back. They both knew why she'd come and there'd be no getting rid of her. The TV was on, the cats were curled up by the gas-fire, and his egg-and-fried-bread was all ready to eat on its blue plate. He couldn't very well say he was 'ill' when he was obviously living the life of Riley. 'Er, have a seat,' he offered, pulling a chair out.

'Thank you very much. Now, get on with your lunch,

while it's hot.' She couldn't resist organizing people, even on their own territory.

Frank cut his fried bread up obediently and poured HP sauce on. 'Would you like a cup of tea?' he said. 'I've just made some.'

People like the Manning-Sanderses no doubt had 'drinks' at dinner time, but he'd only got Dad's medicinal whisky in the front-room cabinet.

'Thanks very much,' she said taking a cup and sipping. 'Mm, you make an excellent cup of tea, Frank.'

Madge had said that too. It was obviously his role in life, brewing up for middle-aged women.

'I wanted to speak to your father,' she began. 'I rang three times this morning but no one answered.'

'No. Well, he's out like, he's doing a temporary job for Morland's Electrical, in Leeds. Fred Huggett got it for him.'

'I see. But you were in, weren't you?' and she give him one of her stares.

'I – I was nervous of answering,' he stammered, 'in case it was someone from the newspapers. My dad's made a right fool of himself with them; you know how they twist things.'

'Very sensible, Frank,' she said approvingly. 'But what I wanted to know was whether he'd kept those letters he received from Brian Brocklehurst.'

'You mean the manager at Shorrock Street? Oh yes, he's got all them in a file.'

' "Those" Frank, not "them". Good. Well, will you ask him to hang on to them please?'

'What for?' he said suspiciously. Maggie had assured him that it would all 'blow over', but it didn't sound as if it was going to, now.

'It's not really for me to say,' she told him, helping herself to a second cup of tea, 'but I will tell you, in strictest confidence, that our friend Mr Brocklehurst hasn't been very satisfactory as a sub-branch manager. It's not *what* you say to customers, Frank, it's *how* you

173

say it. Your father, in, er, doing what he did, making a dramatic statement like that, has drawn much-needed attention to this whole vexed area of bank-customer relations. "Nothing is too small for our listening ear" – I expect you've seen Jack's TV commercial? Well, it should mean what it says. Oh yes, since the story appeared in the papers the Manchester offices have been getting quite a few complaints from Darnley people. They took the Brian Brocklehurst treatment lying down, but your father spoke out. I rather admire that.'

'But will the Friendly Northern take action?' Frank said. Mrs Manning-Sanders seemed to be making out that Dad was a bit of a hero but the law wouldn't see it like that.

She looked rather uncertain, then she said slowly, 'I can't promise, but my husband thinks not. Oh, I'm sure some agreement can be reached without the whole thing snowballing, Frank. It was just a very great pity that the newspapers got hold of it.'

'I expect you think my father's a fool,' he said bleakly.

'Not at all,' she replied crisply, 'though it was certainly, well, an *unusual* course of action to take.'

'Original,' Frank interjected. 'That's what Sister Maggie up at the convent thinks.'

'Yes, I agree, *original*. But, as those silly papers pointed out, he was a man under strain, and under strain people can do unpredictable things. It could happen to anybody.'

Frank didn't answer. Putting his knife and fork together tidily, he began to pick crumbs off the tablecloth with a wet forefinger. Her voice, when she'd said that last bit, had been quite gentle, Maggie-like almost. He'd definitely misjudged her, dismissing her as an interfering snob who wanted to be First Lady of Denning. She'd obviously thought quite hard about the plight of the Tanner family. And just how long had she known that he lived in Bailey Street? Quite a long time, he flab. Well, we all do, at our age,' and she patted her stomach coyly.

'Mmm,' Frank murmured non-committally, but his imagination had already clicked into its 'romancing' mode. Was this the beginning of another 'sincere relationship' by any chance? Was it 'Goodbye, Rita' and 'Hello, Madge'?

Well, his father might do worse, he reflected, waving goodbye and going back into the house. She was neither young nor beautiful, but then, neither was Dad. And his bones told him that Madge Shiplake was the one hundred per cent 'reliable' sort, with her name going all the way through, like Blackpool rock.

Chapter Fourteen

He didn't go to school for the rest of the week. Dad didn't know because he was collected at seven-thirty each morning, and taken to Leeds in Fred Huggett's van. In the evenings Frank went up to his bedroom saying he'd got homework, when he was actually watching videos on Slob's TV.

He might have felt worse than he did about this bit of deceit if only his father had come clean about painting the bank. But it was never mentioned. As the days wore on though, Mr Tanner seemed to get rather more relaxed and cheerful, and Frank decided that Tim's father really must have sorted things out. Then, just after Dad had walked in from Leeds on the Friday, the deputy head-mistress phoned from school to ask where Frank had been for the last three days. Someone had seen him that afternoon, hanging round the new shopping precinct in town.

Mr Tanner threw a fit when he came off the phone. 'You've really embarrassed me,' he shouted, 'I just didn't know how to answer. I don't expect a son of mine to behave like this, you know. When that woman told me you'd been spotted in the precinct, well I . . . What on earth have you been playing at? Do you know it's an *offence*, skipping school? It's breaking the law.'

Frank really let him have it then. 'That's great,' he shouted back, 'coming from you. How do you think I

178

let you see it. It was going to be a little surprise, that's all. Off you go now, and be quick, or I'll start worrying.'

Frank went, blotting thoughts of the new telly out of his mind. Some things were so painful you couldn't really bear to think about them.

Video Scene was in the town centre, in the new shopping precinct. Malc had got his own card now but officially Frank couldn't take films out on it. He wasn't planning to anyhow, it was too expensive and he didn't want to break into his savings. He might not need them to revamp the cellar now though, because Slob was talking seriously about moving into the spare room in Arthur Dunkerley's flat. If he did, Frank would have their bedroom to himself at long last.

Friday night seemed to be video night, and the queue at the counter was very long. No wonder the Essoldo and the Regal cinemas had been turned into bingo halls. Dad was always boring them with tales of how he and Mum used to hold hands in the back row.

As Frank waited for his turn his eyes wandered round the shop. It was quite big and the air was thick with cigarette smoke. Through the haze he could see people browsing through the different 'interest sections': 'horror', 'martial arts', 'comedy shows', 'adult'. The walls were plastered with lurid posters and here and there small TV screens showed selections of the week's 'top ten' films.

The queue shuffled forwards slowly, then he heard the woman up at the till chatting to somebody. 'Got yourself a video machine then, Mr Wainwright? I knew you'd fall eventually. Well, it's a lot of money to lay out but it pays off in the end. It's cheap entertainment, I think. Now, how many are you taking? Right, that'll be three pounds fifty.'

'These two are for Jackie,' the customer said. 'She's four next month. Do you think they're suitable?'

A pause, then, 'Oh, yeah, she'll love these, Mr

Wainwright. We've got a good kiddies' section, haven't we? She's going to have a nice weekend by the look of it.'

'Yes. She's thrilled about the video. Tat, ta then.'

'Bye, Mr Wainwright. Oh, and if we're shut on Sunday night, you can return the films through the letterbox. OK?'

'OK. See you.'

As the man pushed past on his way to the exit, Frank took a step sideways and pretended to examine a display of war films. He'd recognized the voice, from their conversation in the Safari Laundrette. Mr Wainwright was Foxy, the man with the birthmark.

As the shop door banged shut, he saw the small neat head framed in the glass panel. There was no mistaking that pinched, rather scared-looking face, those sticky-out cheeks, that hair, that mark on his neck. Frank, who could never remember what the teachers said in lessons, could remember every detail.

He could remember the cheerless interior at 49 Lime Walk too, and one thing was definite: when Foxy had vacated his chair and gone upstairs with a drink for Jackie, that time he'd peeped through the curtains, there'd been no video recorder hitched up to the television set. He'd obviously got one now though.

Frank brooded about it all evening. Early next morning he screwed up all his courage and went to Wendy News. Lil gave him a very funny look as he came through the door and asked him why he'd not turned up on Wednesday. But she didn't mention Dad and the bank, and she actually said she was glad his 'cold' was better. He did his round in record time, then, on his way home across Larkfield, he found himself going down Lime Walk. He'd known the minute he woke up that day he'd have to check up on 'Mr Wainwright' before very long.

No luck today, though. The blue bike with the kids' stickers was parked in its usual place but all the curtains were shut, and this time there were no useful cracks

182

through which he could spy. But it was still only eight o'clock when he came away; Jackie and her dad were probably still in bed after an orgy of videos the night before. It was always like that when you got something new.

Had the video recorder they'd just acquired really been nicked from the Manning-Sanders' 'drawing-room'? The one way to find out was to get himself inside 49 Lime Walk and check. If it had, 17-10-44 would be scratched along the side with an electronic needle. But supposing he did manage to penetrate Foxy's house, find the magic number and, with it, proof that the man was one of Moira's 'miserable pilferers'? What would he do with the information?

Well, he felt he owed something to Tim's mother, for the way she'd obviously stuck up for Dad and got her husband organized at headquarters. In spite of that row they'd had on the Friday night, Mr Tanner was still being rather cagey about the whole affair. But he'd had a very long phone conversation with somebody that morning and when he'd come through to the back room, where Frank was rearranging the baked-beans carton in its new 'official' position, near the fire, he'd told him the whole thing was 'finished with', and that Frank 'needn't give the whole silly affair another thought'. To celebrate he'd had another tot of medicinal whisky. So it must be true.

'Who was on the phone then?' Frank had wanted to know.

'A Mr Jack Manning-Sanders from head office, and you can't get higher than that.'

'No, you can't,' he'd replied thoughtfully.

'It's an answer to prayer, son,' his father had said piously, draining his whisky glass, though as far as Frank knew, he never said any. 'Answer to prayer' was like 'God bless' and 'have a nice day'. If anybody had been praying for the Tanner family it would have been Sister Maggie. If she had, Mrs Manning-Sanders had obviously responded at her end, and got Jack to pull a few strings.

It was Maggie Frank needed to talk to now, about everything. They'd parted on bad terms the other day and the memory of it still pained him. He'd gone over their conversation so many times in his head, how she'd tried to be patient and understanding with him and how he'd thanked her by yelling that she didn't 'understand'. She must have been really upset because she'd got hold of him and given him a good shake. It must be the nearest thing to violence the walls of 105 had ever seen, walls where Cassie-look-alike madonnas bowed their heads in prayer and Jesus hung patiently on his cross over the Aga.

Only now, when he thought about it from her angle, did the light begin to dawn about smelly Eric, and why she'd done things like washing his feet and mopping the floor after his 'accidents'. He was a heavy drinker and her father had been one too, so bad he'd needed to be fetched home from the pub every night. Drink had killed him off, most probably.

So in doing these menial tasks for Eric, Maggie had really been doing them for him.

Realizing that made their 'quarrel' seem even worse. He ought to put things right; it was his fault.

And quite apart from pursuing the man with the birthmark, there was Frank's own conscience too. He was a bit of a thief himself, first nicking the photo of Cassie and then that picture from the convent. Could he really carry on with this hunting down of Foxy with those things chalked up against him? He was a big hypocrite. He needed to tell her everything, come clean, and get her to tell him what he ought to do. He was in a total muddle about everything.

But he didn't go round to see her; he was too nervous. Instead, he tried to write her a letter.

At school, it was getting very end-of-termish now, so there were plenty of chances. Most of the teachers were

busy writin...
each day, to d...
much to investigate... had several 'quiet' periods
self, so long as it didn... ked in. Nobody bothered
ting, are you, Marjorie?' what you did with your-
timidly one afternoon, to brazen... 'You're not knit-
back-row brigade.   liwell whispered
                                      Bradshaw of the

'Yes, Miss Halliwell.'

'Well, er, do it quietly.'

Even teachers like her relaxed, towards the ... of term.

In spite of all the acres of free time though, Frank couldn't get anywhere with his letter to Maggie. Every single attempt ended up in the waste-paper basket. In those letters he talked about more or less everything, except about what really mattered. He explained how Malcolm really did seem to be planning to move into Arthur's flat, and that Dad was getting their front bedroom 'professionally' done by Madge's brother-in-law, Ron, who was having a hard time with his business; how another 'sincere relationship' seemed to be on the cards, but did Maggie think a middle-aged traffic warden like Madge was really the right person? He told her that the kittens were coming along nicely and how their arrival seemed to have started the humanizing of Malc the Mok, who was quite civilized to him these days. And he told her how he and Lesley were together again, after their lovers' tiff, that Dad had given him some money to replace the designer clothes, and that they might even get married in the summer.

There was nothing about Tanner family life that Maggie wouldn't have known from those screwed-up letters, but the things he really wanted to say Frank couldn't bring himself to write – that he was sorry he'd nicked the picture, but were they still friends? Had Eric come out of hospital yet and was Blackpool still on? Would she tell him what to do about that video recorder at 49 Lime Walk? Was he 'romancing' again, and if he wasn't, and

it did belong to the Ma... ...ses, ought he to tell
the police about the ... ...e birthmark?
On the Wednes... ...st day of term, Mr Wilson
announced the ... ...the Dewsbury Bequest competition. In thei... ...the hundred-pounds prize had
been won ... ...called Rachel Bix. She'd been cun-
ning, bas... project on the history of Arkwright Mill.
It had ... supplied cotton knickers for half the bums
in L... ...ashire, according to Gran Corcoran. Rachel
...n't put that in her project though. Instead, she'd
concentrated on how the Dewsbury family had put their
money into the mill years ago, and gone from rags to
riches in three generations. She'd even got hold of an
old photo of Miss Jessica Dewsbury, doing a clog dance
in the mill yard.

Tim didn't even get a mention for his 'Nine Standards'
project. On the bottom the judges had written 'Perhaps
a little *too* professional?'

'What's that supposed to mean?' he'd asked Frank
miserably. They were speaking again and Frank was
definitely going to the meatless barbecue. It was all
'blowing over' about Dad painting the bank, just as Maggie had predicted.

'Dunno,' he'd answered. But he did. It meant they
knew that Tim had had too much help from grown-ups.
Well, it stuck out a mile.

To his great surprise, Frank got a cheque for twenty
pounds as a runners-up prize, 'Highly original' it said
on the bottom. 'Pity about the presentation.'

'What's "presentation", do you think?' he said to Tim,
still hardly able to believe it, and tucking the envelope
into his top pocket while the other boy watched rather
enviously.

'That you can't spell, I should think, and that your
handwriting's . . . er . . . a bit of a mess.'

'But it took me hours, copying that lot out. I spent a
whole weekend on it.'

'Listen, you've won a prize, haven't you? What are

Chapter Fifteen

Madge now had the key to Miss Sweeney and Dad went down to meet her there the next morning, to have a proper look at the electricals. He was going to do a complete rewiring job and he needed to work out his costs. Frank went with him, to write down all the bits of information on a clipboard. It was easier with two.

Apart from the chippy there were four shops on South Parade: Miss Sweeney, Wendy News, an ironmonger's and on the end a mini-market called Seven-Eleven, the sort that stayed open when everyone else was closed. There was also a little snack-bar with plastic ferns in the window called Paradise Island.

By eleven o'clock Dad had finished his measuring up and sat on a tea-chest at the back of the empty shop, chatting to Madge. She'd brought a thermos of coffee and some home-made shortbread in a tin. Out of uniform, and perched on a neighbouring box in the shadows, she didn't really look too bad. They seemed to have plenty to talk about anyhow, Frank noticed.

He was staring idly through the window when he saw Maggie walk past with two bulging green Seven-Eleven carrier bags. Tomorrow was Good Friday, the day Jesus was nailed on the cross.

That must be an important day for the nuns, no shopping allowed. She looked loaded down. 'Er, I'll see you, Dad,' he called to the back of the shop. A minute later he was out on the pavement, in front of Paradise Island.

'Maggie,' he said, and he tapped her on the shoulder. His voice was squeaky with nerves, not his normal voice at all. She turned round. 'Why, hello, stranger. Where've you been all my life?' and she grinned.

Inside Frank sagged slightly with relief. It was definitely all right, she'd not given him the brush off. Yet something about her was slightly different. That special light inside her, the thing that made you a human being, hadn't been turned off exactly but it was dimmer today. Suddenly, he knew, without being told, that Eric must have died.

'I tried to phone you,' he said awkwardly, 'but Sister Veronica said you weren't available.'

'No. I've been up at the hospital rather a lot in the last week. Anyhow, poor old Eric won't be going to Blackpool with us, I'm afraid; he passed away last night.'

'I'm very sorry,' Frank muttered, staring down at his shoes. What else could you say, about death?

It had started to drizzle and Maggie wasn't wearing a coat over her habit. But she didn't seem in any hurry to go. She simply stood there on the rain-spattered pavement, looking at him with tears in her eyes. She must feel as if her old dad in Ireland had died, all over again.

There was a box of breakfast cereal sticking out of one of the carrier bags, and a couple of leeks. Frank stared down at it, not wanting to look her in the face. It was still hard to imagine that those nuns at 105 were normal eating and drinking human beings. Did Sister Ursula really get those big choppers of hers to work every morning, crunching through the All Bran?

'Why did you phone, Frank?' Maggie asked.

'Oh, I just wanted to ask your opinion about a few things,' he said, trying desperately to sound casual.

'Go on then, I'm listening.'

He looked nervously along the street towards Miss

Sweeney. Dad and Madge might come out at any minute and see them. 'It's a bit . . . well, it's raining out here.'

She consulted the big man's watch strapped to her wrist, then she peered into the ferny window of Paradise Island. 'Let's go in here for ten minutes,' she suggested. 'We can have a drink.'

Frank had a glass of Coke and a vanilla slice and Maggie had a cup of black coffee.

'I didn't think you'd be allowed to come into a place like this,' he mumbled, custard squishing out of his mouth as he ate his cake.

'Oh yes, now and then. We're not exactly animals in a zoo you know,' and she stirred her coffee in silence, waiting for him to begin.

'Listen, I really am sorry about Eric,' he repeated. But he meant he was sorry for her. What he'd said on the pavement hadn't felt enough.

Maggie said quite briskly, 'Oh, he's better off where he is.'

'And where's that then?' He couldn't imagine a heaven. Gran Corcoran always called it 'the other side'; it felt spooky, somehow.

'Well, better than Blackpool anyhow,' and she started making little hollows in the sugar with her spoon. 'Better than this place too, if you ask me, even if it is called Paradise Island,' and she shook the dust from a plastic fern that dangled only inches above her head. 'So what did you phone about, Frank? I've not got very long, I'm afraid. I'm due back at the house in fifteen minutes.'

But even now he couldn't bring himself to tell her about the picture. Instead he spelt out his dilemma about Foxy Wainwright. At first he didn't name names. He said nothing about Tim's parents helping Dad, or about where Foxy lived, just that he thought he might be 'on to something', but that he wasn't sure he should follow it up. 'What would you do, Maggie?' he said urgently, eating the last few flakes of his vanilla slice then pushing the plate away.

191

'Well, first,' she said thoughtfully, 'you've got to be absolutely sure about your facts. You are, are you?'

'Well, not quite . . . not exactly anyhow.'

'OK. Make certain you're right then, without breaking the law of course.'

That was going to be difficult because he'd have to get himself into the house on Lime Walk, but he remained silent.

She seemed unwilling to go on so he prompted her. 'All right, so I make absolutely sure. Then what?'

Maggie paused. 'Well, tell me this, Frank, what's in it for you? I mean, why bother, what's your motive?' Would it earn you any money, for example?'

'It might. But that's not the reason, honestly it's not. Listen, if you must know, I think I've found out who nicked that video from the Manning-Sanderses, and Tim's mother did Dad a really good turn over the bank thing. She's getting dead steamed-up over her neighbourhood watch scheme now; it's driving the whole family bananas. It's just something I could do for them, that's all.'

'I see. And would you give the money away, if you got it? Or would you keep it?'

He opened his mouth to say no, then shut it again. Fifty quid was a lot of money to him. Added to the twenty pounds he'd won, he could get quite a few things for his new room.

'I'm not sure,' he said uneasily.

'Well, whatever you decide, make sure of your facts first, otherwise you could land yourself in trouble.' She stood up and pushed the All Bran box down firmly into the carrier. Then she added, 'If you do decide to go through with it, perhaps you should ask yourself what effect it might have on people, if the police were brought in.'

'On me, you mean?'

'On you and all the other people,' she said mysteriously. 'It's quite a thing you'd be taking on, going to the

192

police. I'm not sure Mrs Manning-Sanders quite thought it through, when she asked Tim and his friends to help.'

'I know,' he muttered. 'I probably won't do anything anyway.' She'd not said so, but she obviously disapproved totally. He felt more confused than ever now.

'Anything else?' she said, buttoning up her purple cardigan.

He hesitated. It was his very last chance to confess about the picture. 'Well, I won a prize for that project. I was only a runner-up, but I got twenty pounds.'

She brightened immediately. 'Twenty pounds? *Only* a runner-up? That's *great*, Frank. And what did your Miss Halliwell say?'

'Oh, she just rabbited on for a bit, like she usually does. She was quite pleased though. So, wouldn't you do anything then, about this man? And the video?' She'd reached the café door now and he'd still not owned up.

'Well, *I* wouldn't, but then, I'm not you, am I? All I'd say is that people who live in glass houses shouldn't really throw stones, Frank. I'll let you know about Blackpool, anyhow.'

'But we won't be going now, will we?'

'Why not? Some of us could do with a day out, we've just done all that spring-cleaning. Do you fancy taking Sisten Ursula on the Wall of Death?'

Frank didn't. She might lose her teeth.

She was just opening the door when he called out, 'Maggie, have you got another five minutes?' He couldn't let her go yet; the conversation wasn't over. She *knew*.

She came back, sat down again and rested her chin on her hands; then she looked him straight in the eyes.

'I took that picture,' he said.

'I know.'

'And I nicked a photo from Tim's bedroom as well, one of Cass. I can't give it back either, it got ruined in the washer at the launderette; it's gone all pink.'

Maggie smiled but it didn't feel like a laughing matter

to Frank. Now he'd confessed at last, the sheer relief of it made him want to cry. She was obviously waiting for him to go on, but he couldn't. He just sat there, pushing a tomato-sauce bottle round in a circle with his finger, staring at the table-top.

'We thought you'd probably got the picture,' she said gently.

'We . . . you mean Sister Geraldine and everybody?'

'Oh yes, we talked about it, all together.' She didn't add 'and we prayed', but he knew they must have.

'And what did you decide?' he got out awkwardly.

Maggie shrugged. 'Only that you must have had your reasons, Frank. I expect it was a sudden impulse, wasn't it? You were thinking about your new room and how you wanted to do it up, and I don't suppose you've got anything quite like that at your house, have you?'

'No,' he said in a whisper, 'no, we've not, and it was so . . . beautiful. I just, suddenly . . .'

'It's all right, Frank, it really is all right. You've had Our Lady looking down on you anyway, while it's been at your place.'

'No, I've not. I wrapped it in a plastic bag and hid it in the cellar. I brought it back twice, but the first time you suddenly decided we'd go for a walk and I somehow couldn't find the right moment to give it back. Then I brought it again, when I came to tell you about Dad painting the bank, but then . . . then . . .'

He was very near to tears now. Maggie saw, put out her hands, and took his into them, her small, chapped, work-worn fingers wrapping round his long thin bony ones, holding them tight. 'If it were only ours to give, Frank, you could have that picture. Sister Geraldine said so herself, it wasn't my idea. Only we can't, you see, because it belongs to the Order. It isn't that it's old and rather valuable, it's just not ours to give. Otherwise we'd have given it to you, honestly.'

Frank closed his eyes tight and made an almighty effort, but in spite of everything the tears rolled down. Maggie held his hands tighter and there they sat, in Paradise Island, a newspaper boy and a nun, but a nun who, just for that moment, stood not only for his father who loved him so very much, or for his mother, who would have loved him, had death not taken her away, but for God himself whose love went on, in spite of what people did, pouring itself out like the man in the Bible, filling a bucket to overflowing with golden grain. He ought to be grateful to poor Miss Halliwell. She'd told them that story, and about Mary Magdalen too, and about the bad woman whom they'd brought to Jesus to be punished.

'Let him who is without sin among you cast the first stone,' he'd said, and they'd all gone off, not knowing what to say. Now Frank didn't know what to say either, though Maggie's message was crystal clear. How could he go running to the police about the man with the stain when he'd nicked things himself? That stealing was a kind of 'stain' too. 'People who live in glass houses shouldn't really throw stones, Frank,' – that's what she'd said. He was in the glass house and no better than Foxy. What was he going to do?

After she'd gone back to Palace Road, he sat on for a bit in Paradise Island, had another Coke and thought about it. He'd *got* to find out if he was right about Wainwright. But if he was, and the video had been stolen, what should he do next?

Maggie seemed to be saying 'do nothing', but that meant leaving the man at large, to do more thieving, and that couldn't be right, either.

One step at a time, he decided finally, paying for his Coke and walking out. He'd get into the house on Lime Walk first and see what was what. After that . . . well, perhaps he'd ring Maggie, report back and talk about it a bit more. It would be easier for them both, probably, after him crying in Paradise Island, easier if there was a gap, so they could both sleep on it.

'Sleep's your best investment, son.' That was one of Dad's little sayings. If it hadn't been for Dad's crazy antics with the green paint, he reflected, walking down the road, he'd have never got so close to Sister Maggie.

It was funny how very good things could come out of very bad ones.

Chapter Sixteen

It was eight o'clock on Easter Saturday morning and he'd finished his round. 49 Lime Walk wasn't on his list, but he would need a valid excuse if he was caught on Foxy's premises. So, just in case, he'd stuffed some copies of the latest *Spotlight* in his orange and banana delivery bag, and here he stood at last, trying to look 'official' on the man's front doorstep.

Nobody was in. The motor bike with the stickers was missing and through the kitchen window at the side of the house he could see breakfast dishes stacked in a sink. You couldn't be too careful though so he went round to the front door and posted a *Spotlight* through the letter-box, making a lot of noise about it. Then he waited. Nobody came down the hall to pick it up off the mat. Wainwright and his little daughter were safely out for the day.

He went to the side door again, took Malc's plastic Video Scene card from his pocket, inserted it into the slit between the lock and frame then jiggled it about, like they did on TV. After a minute or two he heard a little click. He pressed, the door swung open and he stepped inside.

He'd already seen the minute kitchen through the window. It was the sitting-room he wanted to inspect; he pushed down the plastic handle of the connecting door and went straight through.

It was exactly as he'd remembered, the three black plastic 'easy' chairs, the scrap of carpet, the bookcase full of tatty paperbacks, the twenty-inch telly in pride of place in one corner. But underneath the set there was now a black video recorder with some Video Scene boxes stacked on top of it. Feeling slightly sick at the sheer enormity of what he was doing he knelt down, pulled it towards him and looked along the left-hand side. There, in minute silver figures, he read '17-10-44'.

Very carefully, he pushed it back into place again and stood up. But the sudden movement had drained the blood from his head and he felt dizzy. Swaying about, he clutched at the fake stone mantelpiece for support. In the middle of the ledge there was a small bookshelf painted blue. According to the neat white letters underneath it contained 'The Complete Tales of Beatrix Potter', and there was a gap at one end where someone had removed a book.

He was staring at it, waiting to get his balance back before he checked inside for Cassie's name, when there was a little noise behind him. Somebody else had come into the room.

He turned round and saw a child standing in the doorway. She wore a red dressing-gown and red slippers with pink pom-poms on them. One hand was in her mouth, its thumb being sucked vigorously. The other clutched a small square book with a white cover. It was *The Tale of Peter Rabbit*.

Frank took half a step towards her then knelt down. Little kids tended to get frightened if big grown-ups towered over them. 'Hello,' he whispered very gently, 'and what's your name?'

She stared at him, her brown eyes suddenly huge with fear. She was only three years old yet the terrified little face had a haunted, weary look. It was a strangely grown-up face, a face that didn't belong to this minute child's body, clad in its fluffy red. It was the face of someone who already seemed to know about grown-

198

up pain and unhappiness, when all should have been sunlight and simple joy.

Frank stretched out his hands towards her. He thought it was criminal, leaving a child as young as this alone in a house, even for five minutes. But she backed away whimpering, and hid her face behind the little white book.

Then she let out a single, ear-splitting scream, '*Daddy!*' and made for the stairs, tripping over the long dressing-gown as she tottered off, before falling over in a little heap in the doorway. 'Daddy!' she screamed, even louder this time, then she dissolved into hoarse gulping sobs.

Over his head, somewhere towards the back of the house, Frank heard a sudden rush of water, as if some-body was emptying a bath. Then an upstairs door opened. 'I'm coming, love,' someone shouted. 'Just let me get a towel on . . .', and the man with the birthmark came thumping down the stairs half naked, to pick his daughter up off the hall lino.

A few seconds later Frank, his heart pumping so vio-lently he wanted to be sick, was leaning against the brickwork outside the kitchen door, taking deep breaths in an effort to calm himself. Down the garden path he could now see the blue motor bike. Its front wheel was missing and tools were scattered on the path. Through the door, which was still half open, he could hear Jackie being comforted.

He took a silent step sideways, twisted his head round and looked in. Foxy was sitting in one of the black plastic chairs, his wet back turned on the inter-connecting door, with the little girl leaning on the wooden arm, still giving little sobs. 'Let's have a look at this,' he was saying. 'It's all right now, Daddy's here. What? Yes, that's like yours, isn't it? Now listen . . . *Once upon a time there were three little rabbits and their names were Flopsy, Mopsy, Cottontail and Peter . . .*'

Half-way across Larkfield his bike chain broke again. He would have cursed it normally because it was a very long walk back to Bailey Street. It didn't matter today though. He needed time to sort things out, in his mind.

Even in the desolate avenues of the huge estate it felt as if spring had arrived at last. Soft fresh grass was pushing up between the broken pavings, sooty hedges were slowly lightening with new green, and in the rubbish-filled front gardens the thin pale sheaves of daffodil buds peeped bravely out. Frank walked along slowly, sniffing the air, with that picture of Foxy and his little girl stamped for ever in his mind, thinking about human love.

It was a very strange thing, he'd decided, and it had a strange hold over people. The man at 49 Lime Walk was a thief, he'd got proof of it now, and at one time he'd actually suspected him of being the Larkfield Killer too. But whatever the man had done and whatever he was, Frank knew beyond all doubt that what mattered most in his life was that little child. He'd certainly have killed anyone who'd threatened her, that hollow-faced three year old whose deep eyes had seemed to spell out, as her gaze met his, all the troubles of the world. There was obviously no mother any more.

He knew, now, that he had to do something but that it wasn't to go running to Maggie for advice. He would choose his moment – not tonight at the barbecue but next week perhaps – and tell Tim's mother. A week ago he'd never have considered such a thing but everything was different now, he felt he knew her rather better. Underneath that thrusting bossiness Moira cared about things, and he thought she'd be really sad when she knew about that little girl, watching cartoons on their video and reading the Beatrix Potters. Stealing those might be the only stealing Wainwright had ever done, anyhow, and he'd not done it for himself. It didn't make it right, but it made it easier to understand. That's what he was going to explain, if he could.

What Mrs Manning-Sanders did when she knew about it was her affair, though if she did have a big reaction and did tell the police, what would happen to that child? As he pushed his bike along, he could hear the father's voice again, spelling out the story of Peter Rabbit, calming her down with a voice of real love.

Love had blossomed at home too. Every day he watched in fascination as the two kittens grew stronger and bolder, fiercely guarded by their mother who seemed a new creature now, older and very dignified as she carried out her daily duties, washing and feeding the tumbling scraps of fur. And love had somehow brushed off on Malcolm and Lesley. If the kittens hadn't been born in that drawer, he reckoned they might never have got together again properly. Malc was quite protective towards the kittens these days, no doubt because he knew Lesley was watching him closely. Love could achieve some amazing things.

The love Maggie stood for was much harder to understand. The nuns at 105 did things for 'the love of God', like it said on the gate, although God was still a blank to him, unimaginable, unreal. Yet what they did was real enough, taking in thankless old men like Eric who'd done nothing but moan and complain, people who took and gave nothing in return, wanting to give Frank the madonna picture when he'd actually stolen it from them. It was amazing 'love', that was, more than anybody could ever deserve.

On the corner of their street he suddenly stopped, leaned his bike against a fence and went into a phone-box. Calmly this time he dialled the convent number again and this time Maggie herself answered.

'So I was right,' he said, when he'd explained what had happened in Lime Walk, 'but the only thing I'm doing is telling Tim's mother. They're her things, and she ought to know where they are, I think.'

'I agree,' Maggie said, after a short pause, 'only, in a

way, I hope they can sort it out without bringing the police in. That little girl . . . it's not fair.'

'Thought we weren't supposed to use that expression?' Frank said cheekily, an unexpected happiness suddenly flooding through him. 'You told me off once, for saying things weren't fair.'

'I certainly did, and you mustn't,' she told him firmly. 'Listen you, you're going to next-door's party tonight, and then Blackpool on Tuesday, with us. Your dad's found what sounds like a really great girlfriend, so he's happy, and Malcolm's moving out. *And* you've won twenty pounds, for your project. I think you should count your blessings, Frank Tanner, especially when you think of those people on Lime Walk.'

'I do, I *am*,' he said hastily. 'I was just –'

'All right then, see you tonight in your glad-rags.' And she rang off.

As he walked towards Number 14, a white van drove past him, slowed up and stopped on the double yellow lines outside the front door. Then a man got out and knocked. Across the back of the van it said 'Ron Shiplake, Painter and Decorator.' It must be Madge's brother-in-law, coming to give an estimate for the 'Rolls-Royce job' in the front bedroom. It was marvellous. Now Slob was moving in with Arthur Dunkerly till he married Lesley, Frank would have the whole place to himself. He wouldn't need to join the frogs in the cellar, or save up for damp treatment.

He pushed his bike past the house and waved at the front door. Madge and Dad were standing on the step, telling Ron where he could park his van. 'Cup of coffee, Frank?' Madge shouted, 'and I've brought a few rock cakes.'

'I'll just put this in the shed,' he shouted back. 'The chain's bust again.'

Before going inside he stopped and peeped through the back window. The small sitting-room was ten-deep in people. Dad and Madge were arranging cups and saucers on the table; Ron was holding up some blue wallpaper for general approval; Lesley and Slob were sprawled on the settee in a loving tangle with Flump 2 crawling about on top of them, trying to get comfortable. By the gas-fire, in her baked-beans carton, Flump 1 was washing her kittens.

Madge saw his face pressed against the window and waved the electric kettle. 'OK, Frank?' she mouthed.

'OK.' Coffee gave him wind but he'd better have some today, just to show willing. It looked quite a family party in there.

Brother-in-law Ron was still admiring his blue wallpaper. Frank didn't want that in his new bedroom, it was a bit bright and cheap-looking. He'd waited long enough for a room of his own and now it was going to be just right.

Good paper cost money, though. Still, he did have twenty pounds extra towards it now. Dad had been really pleased about him winning that runners-up prize.

The sun came out as he put his hand on the back-door latch, and he suddenly knew it was going to be a very good day. After his coffee he'd have a long hot soak in the bath. Then he'd get his 'glad-rags' out, ready for tonight's party. Maggie and Cass would be there so he wanted to look his very best. He felt Cass was just a friend now; Maggie would always be a very *special* friend.

In the afternoon he was going shopping with his father, to buy something for Tim's mum. Dad said you had to take little presents to the hostess at a party, it was the thing to do. This would be quite a big present, Frank suspected. It would be his father's way of saying thank you, for how the Manning-Sanderses had stuck up for them over the bank episode.

He went in to have his coffee then get ready for his party, but not before taking another last peep at the cheerful scene inside. Dad looked so happy with Madge, and Lesley, fiddling with her engagement ring, looked happy too. She had just given Malc such an adoring gaze it had made her almost pretty for a minute. Flump 2, having given up trying to get comfy on top of them, had joined his family in the baked-beans carton and they were all going to sleep.

Maggie was right to make Frank count his blessings. He really had quite a few.

Some other Puffins

WHO IS FRANCES RAIN?
Margaret Buffie

It's going to be a long hot summer for Lizzie. This year the whole happy family, including her mother's new husband, are going to stay with her grandmother on the lake, usually the highlight of the summer. She decides to get away from everyone and all their bickering, goes exploring by herself and makes a few discoveries which make this summer more exciting and memorable than any other.

THE SECRET IN MIRANDA'S WARDROBE
Sheila Greenwald

Miranda is a solitary child, but her mother is outrageous and always out socializing. When Miranda finds a beautiful old doll she turns her wardrobe into a secret home for it, and gains confidence through playing with the doll — and her lonely life begins to change.

TIMEPIECES
David Leney

A cycle of stories — one for each month — about the lives of contemporary people, young and old, in a small Suffolk village. A strong sense of the passing year emerges, giving a delightful insight into the dramas enacted by the various children and their families. There is the race between two boys to find a missing tortoise, a family's stay in a beautiful country house only to discover that it is not the earthly paradise they had supposed, a story about conker fights and bullies, the death of a family pet, a disastrous school trip, and an amusing misunderstanding over a dead man's Wellington boots.

PARK'S QUEST

Katherine Paterson

When Park visits his dad's father's family he discovers many things which his mother had failed to reveal to him. It comes as a surprise to discover that his Uncle Frank is married to a Vietnamese woman who has a daughter called Thanh. Then Park sees a photograph of Thanh's mother with an American airman, and things begin to fall into place . . .

BAGTHORPES LIBERATED

Helen Cresswell

In the seventh book about the eccentric Bagthorpe family, Mrs Bagthorpe is determined to liberate the female members of the household from domestic drudgery, and sets out to rally support for her radical views. But a string of hilarious incidents proves all too clearly that if there is one thing Mrs Bagthorpe can never be, it's liberated.

ME, JILL ROBINSON
AND THE CHRISTMAS PANTO

Anne Digby

Jill and her family move from London to a new town – new house, new school, new friends. Jill soon becomes best friends with Lindy Hill, the madcap daughter of the town's mayor. Sarah meets the youth club leader, Roy Brewster, and the youth club quickly becomes the centre of the family's activities.

DOWNHILL ALL THE WAY
K. M. Peyton

The chance of a school skiing trip to France means different things
to different people. Nutty and David can't wait to go. Jean isn't sure
about it, and Hoomey is not keen at all. But eventually they do
arrive in the ski resort of Claribel, and their experiences as first-time
skiers make hilarious reading.

SNAPS KELLY
AND THE PAPER MONSTERS
Joseph Ducke

Snaps Kelly lives with his decidedly eccentric grandpa in an equally
eccentric house in London. Snaps is a fairly ordinary boy, until one
hot summer the paper monsters arrive! Suddenly he has to become
an ace detective, determined to discover why all the paper in
London is dissolving. With no newspapers, no underground tickets,
no toilet paper(!) and worse still, no money, daily life is changing
dramatically. Meanwhile, the evil Dr Chengappa is always one step
ahead and it looks as though life in the civilized world could be
changed forever.

A PACK OF LIARS
Anne Fine

When Laura's teacher sets up a pen-pal scheme, Laura finds herself in
correspondence with an extremely boring girl called Miranda. Desperate, Laura decides to liven things up by pretending to be a Lady
Melody from a noble and wealthy family. Her friend, Oliver, is
horrified at her pack of lies and makes her feel so guilty that she
tries to make amends by visiting her pen pal personally, only to
discover that Miranda is a professional thief who steals from the
rich to give to the poor! The plan to expose her makes entertaining
and gripping reading.

Helen
—×—